"I want the truth, Cassandra."

"I meant every word." She gave a choked little cry and tried to break away.

Matthew held her hard. "Sorry. I'm not buying it. I suppose the two of you laughed yourselves sick at your boldness."

"Did you think my letter bold?" A stab of deepest anxiety pierced her. She had tried so hard to get it right.

"It would have been a beautiful letter. From a stranger. Not from *you*." He stood proudly, unsmilingly, cleft chin upthrust.

Her spirits lifted. A *beautiful letter.* "I'm like you, Matthew. I want a life. I want a husband, family. I'm longing to live my dream—"

"So you said in your letter." He cut her off. "The brutal fact is you'd hate every moment of living Outback."

Margaret Way takes great pleasure in her work and works hard at her pleasure. She enjoys tearing off to the beach with her family on weekends, loves haunting galleries and auctions and is completely given over to French champagne "for every possible joyous occasion." Her home, perched high on a hill overlooking Brisbane, Australia, is her haven. She started writing when her son was a baby, and now she finds there is no better way to spend her time.

Books by Margaret Way

HARLEQUIN ROMANCE®
3391—A FAULKNER POSSESSION
3427—BRIDE IN WAITING
(one of two short stories in *Husbands on Horseback*)
3455—GEORGIA AND THE TYCOON
3476—HOLDING ON TO ALEX
3507—BERESFORD'S BRIDE
3532—GABRIEL'S MISSION
3540—BOARDROOM PROPOSAL

    HER OUTBACK MAN
(part of Harlequin's *The Australians* miniseries)

Don't miss any of our special offers. Write to us at the following address for information on our newest releases.

Harlequin Reader Service
U.S.: 3010 Walden Ave., P.O. Box 1325, Buffalo, NY 14269
Canadian: P.O. Box 609, Fort Erie, Ont. L2A 5X3

Mail-Order
Marriage
Margaret Way

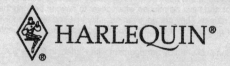

TORONTO • NEW YORK • LONDON
AMSTERDAM • PARIS • SYDNEY • HAMBURG
STOCKHOLM • ATHENS • TOKYO • MILAN • MADRID
PRAGUE • WARSAW • BUDAPEST • AUCKLAND

ISBN 0-373-03551-9

MAIL-ORDER MARRIAGE

First North American Publication 1999.

Copyright © 1999 by Margaret Way Pty., Ltd.

CHAPTER ONE

WHEN he reached the top of Warinna Ridge he reined his bay mare a few short of the cliff face. This was a favourite aboriginal resting place when on walkabout and a magnetic spot for him, too; the best vantage point on the whole of Jabiru. From the high elevation he could look down on the herd scattered over the shimmering, wonderful, emerald-green valley. From umber to emerald. All it took was a drop of rain. Only this time they got a mighty deluge courtesy Cyclone Amy. Danger was a woman, didn't they say? Now the danger had passed.

The rich-coated Brahmans with their distinctive floppy ears, dewlaps and humps didn't have to walk anywhere to graze. The country all around them was in splendid condition now that the floodwaters had withdrawn. Paruna Creek and the Oolong Swamp, home to countless waterbirds, pelicans, swans, ducks, brolgas, magpie geese, the jabirus, the large tropical storks that gave the station its name, were running a bumper and the cattle grazed face-high in rippling pastures. Blue and green couch, para grass, spear grass, you name it. The richest green feed any herd could need to thrive and fatten.

Deep pools of water like miniature lagoons glittered in the metallic noonday sun, a heat haze rising off the surface creating an illusion of hot mineral springs. The pools were everywhere, natural cooling-off spots for the herd, numbers of them wallowing in the silver lakes.

Cherish the earth, he thought, some of the restlessness in his mind quietening as he looked out over a vista that ravished the eye. It was still very hot and humid but a light aromatic breeze scented so sweetly of sandalwood cooled his dark-tanned skin. Though he had a million and one other things to do, it was hard to tear himself away. He looked for a long time, drawing strength from the land. Jabiru filled him with such a sense of pride, of achievement. Not bad for a kid born on the wrong side of the blanket. Nevertheless he felt the taste of bitterness on his tongue. Maybe he would never get rid of it.

The distant hills, spurs of the Great Dividing Range that separated the hinterland from the lush coastal strip, glowed a deep pottery purple, the colour the Aboriginal artist Namitjira had used so wonderfully. An extraordinary brilliance lay over the land. It gave him infinite pleasure. A compensation for the loneliness and isolation. Sometimes at night on long rides under the stars he felt at absolute peace. That wasn't easy for a man like him. Not that Jabiru was a glamour property. It was a lean commercial operation geared for results.

Jabiru cattle were becoming sought after now. But, God, it had taken years and years of backbreaking toil. Now, when he was starting to realise the rewards, he had no one to share it with. Not a soul. There had only ever been him and his mother. Going from town to town. Never staying long enough anywhere to be accepted, until they had come up to tropical North Queensland, over a thousand miles from where they had started, where no one went hungry or cold.

Abundant tropical fruit dropped off the trees, superb beef was cheap, the rivers and the glorious blue sea teemed with fish, and the weather ranged from halcyon to plain torrid.

He'd been around twelve at the time. A difficult age for a boy. At least it had been for him, his mum's protector. His mother, always so very pretty but so soft and vulnerable, had found permanent work helping out in a pub. Marcy Graham, the publican's wife, had taken the two of them under her wing. A good sort was Marcy. The sort that prompted the accolade "heart of gold." They had even lived at the pub for a time until Marcy found them a bungalow they could afford on the outskirts of town. It had been lonely but beautiful on the edge of the mysterious, green rainforest. He even got used to the snakes, mostly harmless. His mum never did.

It had taken a long time to make friends at the local school. Something about him made the other kids keep their distance. He had a wicked temper for one thing, mainly because he wouldn't take the least little gibe about his mother or him. And there had been plenty in those early days. He was tall for his age and strong. It had only taken a couple of fights for the bully boys to get the message.

It wasn't until he was around fourteen and the efforts of the school principal had paid off he found himself with the reputation for being "clever." He didn't know how it happened. He had missed out on so much schooling moving around, yet when he decided to throw himself into it—after all it was he who had to look after his mum—he took off like a rocket. He had graduated from high school with the highest score of any student, giving him the pick of the universities when places were hotly contested. Hell, he could even have become a doctor, a scientist, or a lawyer, only there was no money for all that stuff.

"It's a shame!" Bill Carroll, his old headmaster, told his mother, bewildered to be so confronted. "Matthew could have a great future. He could be anything he sets his mind to."

Only he was a cattleman. And hell, he enjoyed it. He thrived on it. Even when he was living a life of near slavery he'd been happy. He hadn't been able to realise any dream of university but he'd brought the brain and the spirit of an achiever to bear on all his endeavours.

It was Marcy who found him a job as a jackeroo on Luna Downs. Filthy rich absentee owner, swine of a manager. Absolute swine: he had made all the young guys' lives hell, but he got square for all of them before he left.

Once he was old enough—he was plenty strong enough—he bought a very rough slice of scrub with what he thought of then as a hefty loan from the local bank. Somehow despite his youth he had convinced the bank manager he could turn the wilderness into a viable cattle empire. Finally he had sold it three years ago for a handsome profit, launching a full-scale assault on Jabiru.

Jabiru was owned by the Gordon family. In their heyday the Gordons had held significant pastoral holdings, but times had changed. Jabiru had been allowed to run down. Everyone in the business knew it would take a lot of hard work to get it up and running again. Then, everyone knew he wasn't afraid of hard work. It worked for him, too, old man Gordon had taken quite a shine to him.

Of course Gordon knew the story. Everyone did. There were no secrets in the Outback. He was the skeleton in the closet. Jock Macalister's son. Illegitimate son. Difficult to hide it when even he knew he was the image of him as a young man. Sir John Macalister, nowadays referred to as the grand old man of the cattle industry. Macalister had three beautiful daughters but he had never conceived a son in wedlock. Wasn't that sad? He didn't even have a grandson to inherit. The daughters had married, had children. All girls. Perhaps it was the Big Fella up there getting square with Jock's dishonourable past.

His mother had always sworn Macalister had never forced himself upon her. He could have, as he flew around his cattle empire enjoying the traditional *droit de seigneur*. His mother, then working as a sort of nanny on one of Macalister's properties, swore she had wanted him as much as he had wanted her. Only when their relationship was suspected, she found herself shown the road by "The Missus," her immediate employer, who gave her enough money to move far away. Macalister was the Boss; a man with a reputation that needed upholding if necessary by his staff. He was already married to the Mondale heiress at the time. With two small children to think about. Matthew's mother had been young, pretty. In the final analysis—*forgettable*.

He would have been, too, except for his red setter hair, the jet-black brows and his unusually blue eyes. Struth! He even had the same chiselled cleft in his chin. It hadn't taken that North Queensland town a week to uncover their secret.

He was Jock Macalister's kid. Only the rich and powerful Macalisters would never accept that. He had never set eyes on his so-called "father" in his life, though he had seen him plenty of times in the newspapers or on television. He wouldn't actually like to confront the old man. Only Sir John's age would prevent him from being beaten up.

Matthew's own burden in life was grief. Too deep for words. His mother had been killed two years before. She and a few friends had been enjoying a night out on the town, a night which ended in tragedy. His mother and her current boyfriend, not a bad guy, had inexplicably taken a wrong turn. They knew the area well, but ended up in a swollen canal. The dangers of drinking. The car with them in it had been fished out the next day. The same day he had been flown in by the police helicopter to identify the bodies. My God!

"You need to understand your mother, Red," Marcy had tried to console him. "She always felt so alone."

Alone? Who, then, was he? A nobody? He had worked like a slave getting a better home for his mother. It had been far too rough to take her out into the bush. Not that she would have gone. His mother loved people. But he had always provided her with money. Always made the journey into town looking like a wild man with his too long hair and beard, to see how she was faring. She couldn't have been too lonely. There was always a man. A couple of them he had personally thrown out.

His mother had come from England to Australia with her parents as a little girl. All had gone well for some years until her parents split up. She had stayed with her mother who eventually remarried.

"I never got on with my stepfather," was all his mother ever said, but anyone could read between the

lines. His mother, pretty as a picture, was simply a
born victim. It made him feel quite violent towards his
natural father whose life must hide a multitude of sins.

He went by his mother's surname, of course,
Carlyle, and his first name came from the grandfather
in England she remembered with such affection.
Matthew. But no one had ever called him anything but
Red. No one outside his mother who always called
him Matty even when he topped six-two and his body
had developed hard muscle power. Well perhaps there
were one or two others. His old headmaster and a Miss
Westwood who had taught him to love books. Books
were a great relaxation for a man who led a very solitary life. Not that he was a monk. He found time for
women. There always seemed to be plenty but he
picked ones who knew the score. No laying traps for
any vulnerable little girls. And he took good care he
never made one of them pregnant. That would have
been carrying on the sins of his father.

Matthew lifted his battered akubra and raked a hand
through his thick too long hair—heck, it touched the
collar of his denim shirt, then set it back low down
over his eyes. The sun was throwing back searing silver reflections off the serpentine line of the creek and
multiple pools. He had five men working for him now,
two part Aboriginals. Wonderful bushmen, stockmen
and trackers. He wouldn't swap them for the top jack-
eroos off any of the stations. And they were real char-
acters, always ready for a laugh despite the endless
backbreaking work. He had no troubles with the other
men, either, all tough self-reliant, occasionally given
to terrible binges in town when he had to take the four-
wheel drive on the long journey and haul them
back home.

What he needed now was a woman. The right woman. But how the hell was she to be found? He didn't have the time to start up any courting. His life was packed from predawn to dusk and then he was too damned tired to throw himself into the Jeep and drive a couple of hundred kilometres into town. And back. He was thirty-four now. He was well on the way to seeing results, so he kept thinking about starting a little dynasty of his own. From scratch. He had no past anyone wanted to acknowledge. His much-loved and despaired-over mother was dead. He wanted family, he wanted kids of his own. He wanted to make something of his life. Only there would never be a woman he'd force or a child he'd abandon.

Late that afternoon, icy-cold beer in hand, he sat on the veranda of the modest homestead he had built himself, breathing in the pure aromatic air and contemplating his future. Single-storey, the bungalow had its feet planted in the rich tropical earth, a wide veranda that ran the length of the house and a roof that came down like a great shady hat. To him who had never had a real home it seemed like a miracle. It was then as he rocked back and forth, a solution of sorts came to him.

Why not advertise for a wife? Frontier men had had to advertise in the old days. In a way Jabiru was still frontier country. If he kept to what he really *wanted* in a wife he might weed out the empty-headed adventuress or the woman who just wanted to find herself a home.

The idea kept his mind occupied while he prepared himself a solitary but far from don't-give-a-damn dinner. Beef, of course. He ate lots of it and even if the health freaks had cut it out of their diet, the last time he'd seen Doc Sweeney in town he'd been labelled a superbly fit individual. So, grilled eye fillet served up with all the freshly picked salad greens he could lay his hands on.

Aboriginal Charlie, who must have been a Chinese market gardener in another life, had quite a garden going. Different kinds of lettuce, lots of herbs, cucumbers, peppers, tomatoes, shallots—you name it. Waxy little potatoes that came up so clean from the red volcanic soil they only needed a brush off to shine. There were already thirty or more avocado trees on the property that fruited heavily to add the finishing touch.

He didn't allow himself to fall into the habit of eating junk food or those frozen meals plenty of guys on their own settled for. He sat down to a civilised table, a couple of checked tablecloths he got Marcy to buy for him, decent plates.

"Damn it, I'm a civilised man," he told himself. His mother, very dainty herself, had instilled manners in him. He would offend no woman with rough talk or crude ways. Breeding had triumphed, he thought ironically. One day when he could, he would find his mother's family in England. Look them up.

Right now, an enormous gulf separated him from his roots. His maternal grandparents were dead. He knew that much. Strange, his mother had never attempted to go home. Was it pride, or a kind of shame? When he thought about her, which was every day, his heart, or what passed for it, broke. He shook his head. I've got to get a life. And a life means a woman. *A wife.*

CHAPTER TWO

IT SHOULD have been perfect holidaying up here in the blue and gold tropics, but something was missing. It's a long time since I felt good, Cassie realised. Not that it seemed to matter to anyone. Not to her estranged socialite mother who spent her whole life partying and really had never wanted her. She'd had a nanny almost from the moment she was born. A nanny she had come to love until, when she was seven, Rose left.

She had a clear mental picture of herself running into her mother's bedroom after school, her eyes filled with a tearful dread. "Where is she? What happened to her?"

"Don't be tiresome, Cassandra." Her mother, seated at the dressing table, had waved her away. "The usual reason. You're too old for a nanny."

"But why couldn't we say goodbye?" All these years later she could still feel the terrible pull in her throat.

"Why? Because I can well do without your hysterics," her mother had said firmly, turning back to the mirror that showed her elegant reflection in triplicate. "You're growing up now, Cassandra, and you have to move on to a new stage. You're going to boarding school. St. Catherine's, the very best. I expect you to get used to the idea. Daddy and I will be doing a lot of travelling this year. All connected to the business."

Which simply wasn't true. Daddy was a very rich businessman who felt vaguely ill-at-ease with a small girl. Tall, strikingly handsome, seldom at home. But whenever he saw Cassie he patted her kindly on the head then vanished again.

It was a big thing for her, going to boarding school. She learned quickly and, in the end she actually enjoyed it. She made good friends and became very popular both with her peers and the staff. She was head girl in her last year. The top student. That had her parents drooling. With her little successes they moved closer, expressing their pleasure in her achievements. Even better, she had grown from a rather frail, pale child into a highly gratifying reflection of her father's side of the family. Aunt Marian especially, a perennial beauty. There was a general feeling she had turned out rather well.

"It does a child no good at all to smother them with affection," her mother once told her friend Julie's mother, in Cassie's hearing. "Look at Cassie. While Stuart and I were off adventuring, she grew up, became self-reliant."

Julie's mother had smiled back, but the smile never did reach her eyes. Cassie always got the feeling though her mother was always invited everywhere and appeared to have scores of friends, it was just *noise*. No one genuinely *cared* about her. How could they when she had nothing to give?

As soon as she possibly could, Cassie tracked down her darling Rose living quietly in a dreary flat. They had fallen into each other's arms reliving the old grief of separation. She had set Rose up nicely. They couldn't stop her. She was eighteen and had come into a good deal of money, a legacy from her maternal grandmother who had always spoken up for her and was outraged when she was shunted off to boarding school. Grandma had died too early. There had been long-running differences between her grandmother and mother. Mostly about her.

"She might look like me, but honestly I don't know where your mother came from," Grandma often remarked. "Some other planet. Very cold."

Grandma had left Cassie well off. Something that shocked her mother out of her mind. It was a dreadful sin she had been excluded from the will except for a very valuable jade collection she had long coveted.

At university Cassie had a mild eating disorder. Not anorexia or anything like it, but still a bit of a problem. God knows what that was all about, but anyway she got over it. Maybe she'd been trying to take control of her own life. Her own body. Though she did extremely well with her studies, so far as her parents were concerned that was filling in time. Her job was to get married and marry well. Her mother introduced her around relentlessly and found her just the right man. God, he was awful. It was around that time she found the guts to challenge her mother. On *everything*. Instead of shutting up and going away, she found a highly articulate tongue. Heck, hadn't she been a valued member of the University Debating Group?

"What are you trying to do to me, Cassandra?" her mother had cried, off balance with the shock. "You're tearing me to strips."

She had no choice but to leave home. It was never hers anyway. Her mother and herself were very different people. Her father was a benevolent fringe figure. She realised now, in her various relationships since, she had always been looking for a father figure. The men she had gone out with were mostly older, wiser, established in their professions, but alas, no spark, no flame to feed on.

I wish I could share with someone, Cassie thought. I wish I could run into strong comforting arms. I wish I could look at a man with love and respect. Wishful thinking more like it! A consequence of her pretty dreadful childhood. She prayed if she ever became a mother she would know how to show love.

The sun was getting too hot, Cassie noticed now.

She moved languidly off the recliner and stood up. Another dip in the aquamarine pool then she and Julie could start thinking about lunch. Maybe that wonderful little Italian place built on a ridge overlooking the sea. The seafood up here was out of this world, fresh from the Reef waters and straight onto the table. Second thought, pasta. She loved pasta. Who didn't? Hadn't the ancient Etruscans made pasta? The Chinese? Didn't they make *everything?* Marco Polo was supposed to have enjoyed delicious pasta in China. Pasta and noodles were essentially the same thing. Many a time she'd tossed either pasta or noodles with a simple tomato, basil and extra-virgin olive oil sauce.

She was the cook here. Julie, her friend from their very first day at St. Catherine's was almost totally un-domesticated. Sometimes it came with the territory. Cassie herself had barely been inside a kitchen until she had moved out of her parents' house. Her parents had a housekeeper, an excellent cook who presided over her domain jealously. Her father had a full-time chauffeur, as well.

Julie's father, head of the stockbroking firm for which they both worked, was a lovely man. Her mother, who did a great deal of charity work along with the partying, was lovely, too. Lucky Julie! It was their tropical hideaway—really a fabulous retreat—she and Julie were staying at. They were supposed to have come up much earlier, but Cyclone Amy had put a halt to that. They had had to wait a full month before things settled down and the weather returned to glorious. Now they would dress in something easy and go into town.

"Why not try the pub?" Julie suggested when they were out on the sea road. "They have a nice little setup out the back. The food's supposed to be very good. Heck—" she swung her head to admire the splendid produce in one of the many roadside stalls fronting the local farms "—can you believe the tropical fruit? The size and the variety. I don't recognise half of it."

Cassie sat stiffly upright, her face paling. "Goodness, Julie. Watch out!" A station wagon was rapidly approaching them and Julie, in a hired BMW—she didn't know how to drive anything else—was holding the middle of the road like some hooligan playing chicken.

"Sorry." Julie corrected her positioning with a loud gulp that turned into contrite giggles.

"In the interests of survival, I think I'll drive," Cassie said firmly. Julie had developed the very risky habit of turning her head to look at things when she should have been focused on the road. It was more pronounced up here where the scenery was astonishingly beautiful and the sea road was bordered on one side by an almost continuous rampart of blossoming white bougainvillea like great foaming breakers, on the other, the crystal blue seascape. "People like you need a chauffeur."

"Yeah. Like your dad. Spoken to him lately?" Julie asked wryly, knowing full well the answer.

"I plug away but I think he's aware I've gone missing."

Julie shook her head. "You've had a terrible time, Cass."

"Only with my parents," Cassie quipped, but didn't smile. "Pull over, lady." She did her imitation of a traffic cop. "Like *now*." Life mightn't be all that brilliant but she didn't fancy going off one of the steep slopes.

They were both standing at the side of the road getting ready to change positions when a dusty four-wheel drive with a formidable bull bar pulled up alongside them.

"Everything okay?" The driver, a man, lowered his head to look out at them.

Cassie, overcome by an intensity of awareness, stood rooted, but Julie let out a quite audible, "Wow!"

"Excuse me?" One distinctively black eyebrow shot up, mockery laced with a certain amount of mischief.

Cassie predictably was the first to gather her wits. "We're fine, thank you," her breath expelled on a rush of air as she tried to overcome her confusion. "Just changing drivers."

"Well, take care then." Brilliant blue eyes sought and challenged her gaze. "Next time I wouldn't pull up quite so close to the edge. We've had a lot of rain. There could be slippage."

"Many thanks." Cassie gave a quick jerk of her head, wondering why she was behaving like she was.

"No problem." He lifted a hand to her, the intensity of his own gaze undimmed.

The engine of the four-wheel drive started up with a roar, another brief salute and he was off.

They were silent for quite a few moments, then Julie burst out in amazed ecstasy. "Did you see that, Cass? That had to be the best-looking guy I've ever seen in my life. Colouring to die for! Dark red hair, copper skin, jet-black eyebrows, the hottest blue eyes on the planet. Where has he been all my life?"

"Out bush." Cassie was surprised her voice sounded normal. "At a guess, I'd say he's a cattleman on one of his periodic forays into town. The long hair and the physique, the gear."

"Boy!" Julie gave a feline growl. "Talk about ten years searching for my hero. I've found him." She gave Cassie a little punch on the arm. "Sure he wasn't an apparition?"

"I'm hoping not," Cassie laughed, suddenly sounding exuberant.

"So let's get our skates on," Julie urged, running to the passenger side of the car. "It'll take us another twenty minutes to get into town."

They recognised the battered four-wheel drive parked outside the pub. "What did I tell you? The best people eat here!" Julie crowed in delight.

"No." Cassie was surprised by her own reluctance. Normally she might have seen it as a bit of fun. But that guy, stunning as he was, wasn't a man to be trifled with.

Julie stared at her friend in amazement. "If you say you weren't impressed, you're lying in your teeth."

"He's very handsome, I agree."

Julie shook her blond head. "Handsome doesn't say it. I thought I was going to swoon."

"All right, he's terrific," Cassie conceded, yanking the thin strap of her camisole top back onto her shoulder. "But kind of dangerous, didn't you think?"

"As in what?" Julie reluctantly considered it. Cassie was extremely smart. Even her dad said so and he was sparing with the praise. "I thought he was very gallant, stopping like that."

"Well, we're not exactly bad-looking are we," Cassie retorted. "I know he wasn't giving us any come-on, rather the reverse, but he looked pretty complicated, complex, not your ordinary kind of guy. I'd say he's done a lot of living and done it hard."

"Heck, you noticed a lot." Julie, as usual, was impressed. "All I latched onto was the beauty of those *eyes!*"

"I know." Cassie smiled. "I saw the lightning strike. Don't follow it up, Julie. I'm only speaking in your best interests. Guys like that need a sign around their neck—Beware."

"Cassie, don't worry. Trust me." Julie shook her friend's arm. "Everything will be sweet. I only want to see him again. See if he's as stunning as I thought. Probably he'll sound like a redneck as soon as he opens his mouth."

Marcy looked up as the two young women entered the pub. She knew who they were, or she knew the cute little blond one, always laughing, shoulders bobbing, staring around her with wide blue-eyed interest. She was the daughter of the rich couple, the Maitlands, the people who had built a luxury retreat out at Aurora Bay. Marcy, who liked to give people private nicknames, called her Blondy. The other one was Sable.

She'd seen her a couple of times around town. Hard to miss her. Where the little blonde was pretty, her friend totally eclipsed her. Mane of darkest brown into black hair like a luxurious fur pelt so thick it formed a swirling hood around her face. Light, luminous eyes like a river in the rain, polished skin. She was tall and very slender, but healthy-looking, vibrant. The two of them were dressed almost exactly the same. White cotton jeans so tight they looked like they'd been poured on, little-nothing tops that made the most of high young breasts and delicate shoulders. The heads were already turning, as well they might.

To have looked like that even for a day, Marcy thought. "Can I help you, girls?" she greeted them with her wide infectious smile.

"Yes, please." Sable approached. For all her classy look she wasn't uppity. Nice and friendly. "I'm Cassie Stirling. This is my friend, Julie Maitland. We're staying at Julie's parents' place on the point."

As though I don't know everything that goes on in the town, Marcy thought. "Yes, I know, luv." She nodded pleasantly. "Aurora Bay. Big terracotta place on the point."

"That's it!" Julie moved up to join her friend at the counter. "We thought we might do lunch." She had an appealing slightly breathless delivery, but there was a touch of patronising there absent in her friend.

"Glad to have you," Marcy said. 'You're not looking for anyone are you?" Blondy was all but standing on tiptoes looking around.

"You have to understand this is confidential." The girl bent to Marcy with a stage whisper. "We're hard on the track of a gorgeous-looking guy with hair like a dark flame and burning blue eyes. We had an idea he might have come in here.''

''Well, you had the idea.'' Cassie coloured, wishing Julie would shut up.

''That would be Red. Red Carlyle.'' Marcy told them matter-of-factly, picking up a cloth and wiping off the already spotless counter.

''You know him?'' Julie asked hopefully.

''Twenty years and more.''

''Not married, is he?'' Julie asked.

''Funny you should say that.'' Marcy gave them a rather sardonic smile. ''He's advertisin' for a wife.''

''Then that's definitely not the one,'' Sable said.

''There's only one Red.'' Marcy shook her head. ''Matter of fact, the ad is in the local paper.''

''You're having us on, aren't you?'' Julie pulled a little face.

Sable smiled, too, but in a special way, kind of tender, Marcy thought. For some reason Marcy associated smiles like that with people who carried an inner sorrow. Red had a smile like that. Dazzling, lighting up his whole face, but with something that tugged at the heartstrings. At least that's what Marcy had always thought.

''What's wrong with the women of this town?'' Sable was asking with a humorous tilt of her brows.

''A man like that on the loose!'' Blondy rolled her eyes.

''Works too hard, that's his problem,'' Marcy told them. ''How's he ever gonna find a wife when he spends all his time on Jabiru?''

''And may I ask what Jabiru is?'' Blondy spoke in a facetious fashion that didn't do her justice. ''Make sense to you, Cass?'' Looking amused, she turned her head.

"I'm sure it's a property of some kind. A cattle station probably." Cassie gave Julie a little quelling shake of the head.

"Right in one," Marcy announced cheerfully. "Red runs Brahmans. Very hardy breed. They do very well right throughout the North where the British breeds can't survive."

"How interesting," said Julie. "And this—Jabiru, is it *big?*"

"Up here, girlie, we take vastness for granted," Marcy said bluntly. She was starting to tire a little of Blondy, something that wasn't lost on her friend.

"Would you have a table for two free?" Cassie intervened. By now she really wanted to get out of the pub but she was loath to offend this nice, cheerful woman with the smile lines creasing her vibrant green eyes.

"Sure, luv." Marcy reached under the counter and retrieved the local paper folded over to the page that carried Red's astonishing advertisement. She was still trying to take it in. All Red had to do was turn up Saturday night when the pub was full and holler. Chances are he would get knocked down in the stampede. "The one with the ring around it." She stabbed the paper for emphasis. "You can read it while you're waiting for lunch."

The courtyard expanded magically, wonderfully, a cool and shadowy place with masses of flowers in pots, great baskets of ferns suspended from the rafters, latticed walls dripping with a dusky rose bougainvillea, circular tables, green and white bordered cloths, garden chairs. There was a lot of laughter, a lot of talking, with everyone dressed very casually, tourists and locals. It was almost full. Every male to a man gave the girls long appreciative looks. One around their own age raised his hand indicating there was plenty of room at his table. But Marcy ignored him, showing them towards the rear with its green-gold bars of light for all the world like the sun pouring through stained-glass panels.

"This is enchanting," Cassie said, gazing around her with real pleasure.

"We think so, Luv." Marcy was pleased. She and Bill had put quite an effort into getting it right. She stopped at a table for two centred like the others with a bud vase holding a spray of the lovely Cooktown orchid, the State flower. "Anything to drink?"

Both girls chose mineral water with lime.

"You'll find the chef's suggestions posted on the board." Marcy waved a plump arm towards the blackboard. "I'm sure you'll find something you fancy. Coral trout. Red Emperor, straight from the trawler. Gulf prawns big as bananas. We could make up a lovely seafood platter for two if you like. The crab is superb."

"I know, heavenly!" Cassie's mouth started to water.

"Think it over. I'll be back in a few minutes to take your order." Marcy started to move off, then turned. "By the way, Red will be in shortly. He has some business down the road."

The Lord works in strange ways, Marcy thought. The girl, Cassie, with the eyes clear as diamonds and her obviously privileged background, was at a crossroads in her life. There was something missing. Someone. Marcy had a sure instinct about such things. Bill often told her she had the second sight inherited they both thought from her Scottish grandmother. Besides, there wasn't anything she wouldn't do for Red.

Less than ten minutes later as the girls exclaimed over the delicious seafood platter Marcy was setting before them, Red Carlyle appeared at the entrance to the courtyard, instantly creating his own force field. He was greeted on all sides with shouts and waves, lifting an all-encompassing hand in acknowledgment. His gaze ranged over the courtyard for a moment until he caught sight of Marcy's short plump figure. Immediately he began to stride towards her, moving with such grace and pent-up energy, Cassie felt a thrust of excitement in the pit of her stomach. He had such a blaze about him she felt like ducking her head. He was heading towards them, abundant dark red hair swept back, touching the collar of his blue denim shirt. No short back and sides for him. The remarkable eyes glowed turquoise, sweeping over the girls as Marcy moved her body to follow the girls' stare.

"Red!" She greeted him with motherly pleasure.

He smiled and Cassie found herself gripping the arms of her chair. This was the man who was *advertising* for a wife? Why, he was so handsome, so vibrant, it made her eyes smart to look at him. The dark blue gaze was on her now, a long measuring scrutiny, then on Julie, who had her pretty pink mouth open like a fish.

"Well, I see you made it safely into town." He softly shook his head as though he was surprised.

"You know these young ladies, Red?" Marcy executed a double take.

"We passed one another back on the road. Didn't get to names."

"I'm Julie Maitland," Julie piped up, giving her best Drew Barrymore smile. "This is my friend—"

"Cassandra Stirling." Cassie wanted to identify herself.

"*Cassandra?* As in, daughter of Priam King of Troy?" He looked at her with those amazing eyes, the same long steady assessment.

"You'd better believe it," Julie quipped. The original Cassandra had been condemned by Apollo to prophetise correctly but never be believed.

"A beautiful dangerous name for a beautiful, dangerous woman," Matthew responded, seeing a woman he could want badly but was hopelessly out of reach. Her eyes put him in mind of a silver river, the lining lashes as thick as inky-black ferns. Skin like magnolia silk, lovely long neck. Dire consequences were attached to wanting a woman like that and he wasn't a man to long for things beyond hope of fulfilment.

"Red Carlyle." He introduced himself. "I wasn't christened that. My ma called me Matthew after my grandad in England, but it took less than a week to be rechristened up here."

"Gorgeous hair, that's why!" Marcy grasped a handful, fixing him with an affectionate gaze. He towered over her by a good foot. "I was telling the girls, here, you've been advertising for a bride."

Perhaps he would be embarrassed! He wasn't. Unflappable. A touch speculative.

"Sure have. Saves a lot of time. Only *one* thing. The frivolous needn't apply. A serious offer demands a serious response."

Julie raised her eyebrows, plainly dumbfounded. "It's hard to believe any woman could resist you."

He glanced at her and shook his head. "We're talking about a full partner in my business. Cattle ranch, name of Jabiru. I'm talking about a woman who can share my vision. A woman who's strong in her own right. A woman who can give me children we'll both love and enjoy. I'm not talking about a chick who wants to move in and play house. I'm talking about much, much more.''

Julie coughed. ''So this brings me to my application.'' She was only half joking.

He laughed. Warm and deep. His voice far from being country hick was educated, very attractive, with curiously an English accent.

''Write it down,'' he invited. ''No need to send along the photograph. I know what you look like. Pretty as a picture. I know, too, you're joking. You're the daughter of a very successful man and you've been looked after all your life. *Pampered.*''

Julie sighed. ''That's exactly the way my folks raised me. What about Cassie? What do you see in her?'' Julie had already gained the impression of some undercurrent.

He turned his attention to Cassie of the billowing hair. ''Oh, someone who's had sadness in her life at some point. But a person who won't let herself be overwhelmed.''

''Say that's spot-on. Tell us more. Sit down,'' Julie invited. ''Talk to us.''

He shook his head as though he had already said too much. ''Love to. Some other time maybe. I'm on a pretty tight schedule.''

''You have to grab a bite to eat, Red,'' Marcy jumped in. ''I can easily move you all to a larger table.''

''Really, please join us,'' Cassie said with so much

feeling it shocked her. In all her life she had never met anybody to match his shattering impact. Though he was acting friendly, she was smart enough to realise this was a man with a dangerous edge. There was an inner core of aloofness in him, as well, almost an arrogance. Maybe it was just a fiery pride.

"All right, then." He came to a quick decision. "I'm pretty hungry for Marcy's roast lamb. And vegetables, Marcy. Lots of them. I haven't cooked for days."

"You mean, you do your own *cooking?*" Julie, whose pièce de résistance was an overcooked omelette, asked.

"I'm an expert," he answered with no sense of false modesty.

"He is, too." Marcy gave him a proud smile. "His mum started him off and I took over by handing over a few cookbooks. Red, here, lives like a feudal lord."

Pleased with the way things were going, Marcy busied herself setting up a larger table two places down. Matthew, obviously used to helping her, picked up the girls' seafood platter arranged beautifully on a colourful ceramic plate and carried it down. He even went back and picked up the bud vase seeing there wasn't one on the new table. Finally, he seated both girls with a stunningly elegant flourish, before he flung himself into a chair with lavish pent-up grace.

"So, what are you doing up here?" he asked. "Holidaying?"

"Julie's parents have a hideaway up here," Cassie explained, turning her head to face him.

"Hideaway? I bet it's big enough to get lost in," he mocked.

Both girls nodded their assent. "It's on the point at Aurora Beach."

"Hell, I love that place," he said. "I haven't been there in a long time." Although he appeared to be addressing Julie, his eyes kept regarding Cassie as though he sought to commit her features to memory. He even moved his chair to a better angle.

Cassie found it as disconcerting as it was thrilling. She felt overexcited: racing in top gear.

"Jabiru keeps you very busy?" She allowed herself to look into his bronze face and saw chiselled features, a beautiful sensuous mouth, good jaw, cleft chin.

He nodded his handsome, flamboyant head. "It's taken years of my life. Years of backbreaking work to develop it."

"But you treasure it?"

His eyes glittered turquoise. "My Promised Land. The place I feel truly at home."

"Then you're a lucky man."

"I figure I am." He stared at her. So why did he catch that little note of sadness? It didn't make sense. Both of them were undoubtedly young women who lived in a style he could only imagine.

"But to advertise?" Julie had been avidly following their dialogue. "I bet you could get any woman you want."

"I'm thinking you're too kind. Getting the right woman might take a miracle, but I'll keep trying. I live an exhausting life, but soon I hope I can slow down. I'm not getting any younger. Thirty-four. Time to get a life."

Julie laughed. "But surely you know all the local girls?"

"As in saying 'good day,'" he admitted. "I haven't

invited them all out to the ranch.'' The turquoise eyes glinted. ''You'd be surprised that local rag goes far and wide.''

''So how are you going to *know?*'' Cassie asked quietly. She turned her head, pinned by the charge he sent out like an electric thrill. Maybe he even *saw* it, because of what he said.

''A thunderbolt from Heaven.'' His tone was sardonic. ''What do the French call it, a *coup de foudre?*''

''Does it *really* happen?'' Cassie asked from the depths of her soul. She hadn't meant to. She wasn't used to being fascinated by a man. Generally it was the other way about. She the object of desire who turned away.

''I'm *sure* it does,'' he answered in a strange, harsh voice. ''Just as I don't think acting on it would be wise. I'm looking for something less extravagant than a dangerous passion.''

''You have to see you're just the person for it?'' Julie shot him a playful glance.

''No, ma'am.'' Not only did he shake his head emphatically, he waved a dismissive hand. Elegant, long-fingered, darkly tanned, calloused on the fingertips and palms, Cassie noted.

There's a story here, Julie thought, convinced of it.

''Headlong passion can be very destructive. Wouldn't you agree?'' he continued. ''I wonder just how many people have been swept into an ocean of grief. I know it happens.''

''So you're planning a marriage of convenience?'' Cassie asked, a flicker of something very like antagonism in her voice. What was the matter with her? She felt as tight as a spring.

"Hey, it must be convenient, that's for certain. Perhaps something in between. Many cultures have arranged marriages. Had them for many centuries and they seem to work out. Have true worth."

"So you're saying falling love isn't the answer?" Cassie was persisting and didn't know why. If only he'd stop looking at her like that.

"I'm saying many, many love matches end in divorce," he retorted, his enunciation clear. "I've seen plenty of relationships flounder. The woman is generally left to make a home for any children involved."

"Yes," Cassie agreed, then abruptly changed the subject. "So, you're English."

"I'm as Australian as you are." His beautiful eyes stared her down.

"I only meant you have an *English* accent." She had to strive to smile. Her mouth felt dry. "Where did you pick it up?"

"My mother was English," he explained briefly.

"Oh, I see." Cassie realised it wasn't a subject he was going to talk about.

"Actually you sound great," Julie soothed. She could have sworn Red and Cassie were attracted to each other. Attraction with a dash of hostility. No, not *hostility,* she decided, something rather complex.

Marcy returned at just the right moment with Red's roast lamb and a large side dish of vegetables. For a while conversation stopped as they enjoyed their meal. He ate ravenously for a while, Cassie noted. No bad table manners, indeed not, just a man who was totally concentrating on good food. A man who probably had only in recent days been able to grab a meal on the run.

"This is wonderful." He looked up and reached for

his glass of beer. "We've been out on a four-day muster. Didn't stop for long. Pushed too damned hard. The floods have held us up but the country's in fine form now the waters have abated."

"It's like another world!" Cassie gazed at the stupendous hanging baskets of ferns. "I've never seen anything like the vegetation up here. Or the colours! The extraordinary depth and brilliance of the sky, the rich red and emerald earth, the endless white beaches, the sparkling blue sea."

"The Tropics, ma'am," he drawled. "I expect you know many of the islands of the Great Barrier Reef?"

"We know Hayman well," Julie volunteered, daintily downing a creamy rock oyster.

"Of course." Momentarily his lids came down. Hayman was one of the great resorts of the world. A resort for the wealthy.

"Actually I cruised the Whitsunday's with friends," Cassie said, smiling in remembrance of one of the most beautiful and peaceful holidays of her life. "We visited many of the lesser known islands and cays, explored the wonders of the coral reef, the gardens and grottoes, swam in beautiful lagoons. A heavenly blue world of infinite distances."

"Yes, it's glorious," he agreed, spearing the last morsel of roast potato. "So close yet I haven't been able to get away in years."

"You mean you haven't been able to take a *holiday*," Julie asked.

"More important things to do," he laughed. "I'm not complaining. Jabiru's mine and I love it. On the other hand it's good to have the company of two beautiful women." The dazzling eyes flashed over them, brilliant but impenetrable. "Do you know anything about ranching, as the Americans say?"

"Some." Cassie nodded. "I was invited once to a race meeting on Monaro Downs. A huge affair. The place belongs to Sir Jock Macalister," she said casually. "Being a cattleman you're bound to know of him. Monaro Downs is the Macalisters' flagship in the Channel Country."

"I know where it is," he interrupted, startling her with the curtness of his tone.

Colour moved under her high cheekbones. She spoke quietly. "What's the matter? Have I upset you in some way?"

A muscle in the clean line of his jaw jumped erratically. He nearly said yes. Such was her magic. "Not at all. Anyone in the Outback would know of Macalister and his empire. So you were impressed?"

"I sure was," Cassie replied, regarding him with an odd half smile. "I've never seen anything like the homestead. The finest mansion you could imagine set down in a million wild acres. Nothing except for endless miles of plains and towering sand hills. I missed the miracle of the wildflowers. It was the middle of the drought. My parents were lucky enough to witness the spectacle. They said it was unbelievable."

"So you weren't along on the trip?"

"I was at boarding school at the time."

"Boarding school?" One black eyebrow shot up. "I figure your parents must be on the land, as well?"

"My father is a Sydney businessman," she told him quietly. She didn't dare mention his strong business connections with Macalister.

"Nobody heard about day school?" The sensual mouth quirked. "I'm sorry." He gave Cassie a smile that heated her blood. "I have to watch my tongue. You have brothers and sisters?"

"I'm the only one."

"Tell me about it." He shrugged. "I was the only one, as well. And you, Miss Julie?" he addressed her with a light-hearted mockery.

"The only daughter, which I'm happy with. Two big brothers. Cass has been my best friend since our first day at St. Catherine's. A posh school for young ladies."

"You mean you were bundled off, as well?" he asked in amazement.

"No, I was a day pupil. Cassie's parents travelled a lot," Julie informed him.

"And when was this? How old?"

"Not yet eight." Cassie reached over to take Julie's hand affectionately.

"Really." Carlyle shook his head. "It hardly seems possible any parent could part with you. Even *now* the unhappiness is in your eyes, Cassandra."

It was like being caught in a passionate embrace. "Surely not," Cassie managed.

He regarded her with the kind of intensity she was just barely getting used to. "You've got the kind of shimmering eyes a heart's beat away from tears."

She took a deep breath, feeling a very real panic. "I can see I'll have to protect my gaze from you."

"Too observant?" he asked with a mixture of sympathy and challenge.

"No one else has mentioned it." She thought she was losing a layer of skin.

"I'm sure they've noticed." His smile was twisted. "Luminescent, isn't that the word? I didn't get past high school—'' this with a touch of self derision ''—whereas you two got to go to university I'll bet.''

Julie nodded. ''I did what I was told. I struggled through. Cassie is the brain. We both work for my father. He's a stockbroker.'' She didn't add ''big-time'' but she got his full attention.

''That's interesting. I've made quite a bit for myself playing the market. It's amazing what you girls are doing these days. Showing us guys up. All you need is the chance.''

''So, no chauvinist?'' Cassie asked, feeling another great surge of attraction but struggling against it.

He tossed back the rest of his beer. ''No way. Women have resources to call on we guys don't. I know a woman took over the running of a big station when her husband was killed, as tough and intelligent as the best of 'em. Actually I have an intense admiration for a woman's strength. And an intense sympathy for the soft little vulnerable ones some man always treats badly.''

''You're going to make a wonderful husband,'' Julie sighed.

''I'm going to give it my best shot. A commitment is a commitment. Isn't that right?''

Neither young woman was about to argue. If the truth be known, they were spellbound.

A moment later Matthew shoved his chair back, coiled ready to spring into action. ''That was great!'' he said with satisfaction. ''Marcy knows exactly the way to a man's heart.'' He pushed his chair in, a smile deepening the curve of his mouth. ''It's been a great pleasure meeting you, Julie, Cassandra.'' His eyes moved from one to the other. ''But I've got to get cracking. I hope you enjoy the rest of your holiday. Before you go back to your world of luxury."

"No chance of seeing Jabiru, I suppose?" the irrepressible Julie asked.

He was about to shake his head, but suddenly relented. A split second's impulse. "Why not, if you're really interested," he found himself saying, much against his better judgment. "I can't come for you, much as I'd like to. This is a bad time. But by next week the pace should slacken off. If you'd like to make the drive, you're very welcome. But I think that'll put you off," he mocked.

"So, what day next week?" Julie persisted, wanting to follow it up by helicopter if she had to. This guy was something else.

"Ring me," he said, his voice deep and sonorous. "Marcy will give you my number."

God, how dumb can a man get! he thought as he made his way out onto the street. Little Julie with her wiggle was having a bit of fun, he could see that. But what the hell! He was sick of the quiet life. The other one—Cassandra—though she listened to her friend with a mixture of amused affection and dismay, was sending different signals. She didn't look like she wanted to come. There was even a kind of anxiety in her. He had sensed it. Anyway, she was way out of his league. A woman from a world he could never get into. A woman, it now seemed, from Jock Macalister's world. That alone suffused him with a chill, helpless anger. Nothing could be gained from even seeing her again. He regretted, too, ever looking into her eyes. There was a woman he could badly want but never have.

CHAPTER THREE

"WHAT in the world is goin' on, Red?" Ned Croft, his old mate from town, asked him. They were sitting on the veranda enjoying a cold beer and a quick lunch of the fresh bread rolls Ned had brought from the town's bakehouse, stuffed with his own ham, cheese and pickles.

Ned, all of seventy-five, but very fit and wiry with a long bayonet scar on his right arm from the Second World War, often made the trek, lured by his old bush life and the fact that he and Red had struck up quite a friendship, kept glancing down at the swag of mail he had assured Mavis at the post office he would deliver to Red.

"Bloody advertisin', mate. I can't accept that," Ned said, scratching his balding, freckled scalp. "A big handsome fella like yourself could have any girl you wanted. Especially now you've become so successful. It's a great life out here and you've made the homestead real nice."

"I need a wife, Ned," Matthew said, straightening up to pick up another roll. Was there anything better than freshly baked bread and butter?

"You did mention that. But *advertisin'*, mate? Seems utterly wrong for a bloke like you."

"The way I see it, Ned, it will save me a load of time."

"Goin' on that." Ned pointed downwards with a

gnarled thumb. "But what about love, boy? Haven't you given a bit of thought to that?"

Matthew's eyes blazed. "Hell, Ned, I know what love is. I loved my mother. But I've found this romantic love business is a bit of a trap. Sometimes it's over before it's begun. Then there's my background. The past. At least everyone around here knows all about the skeleton in my family closet."

Ned shook his head. Given to lengthy considerations, he didn't say anything for a while. "Don't talk skeletons to me, lad. You're as good a bloke as any girl could get. Better. I know you take this illegitimate bit real serious, but no one else does. You was the victim. The unlucky one. It's Macalister who's the bastard."

"And no argument from me." Matthew grinned. "But some people place a lot of store on family. I remember life with Mum. Moving from place to place. Never having anyone. No relatives. No support group. No damned identity. Even some of the kids at school gave me hell until I found a way to shut their mouths. I have to find an ordinary girl who knows the truth and won't shy away from it."

"Why, did you have someone *else* in mind?" Ned asked shrewdly, turning his bony silver head.

"No," Matthew lied.

"You don't sound sure," Ned replied. "I don't know about this ordinary bit, either. There's nuthin' ordinary about you, Red. Don't you understand that?"

"I'm a realist, Ned. I've come a long way, but now I want to put down roots. Marry a good woman who'll give me a family. I want to build a relationship that will hold us together."

"That's some ambition," Ned, long divorced, said. "That girl, Fiona, didn't you like her?"

Matthew laughed. "Ned, Fiona left town ages ago. She went to Brisbane to find herself a nice solicitor."

"Don't know what she's missin'. Are you gunna read all of these?" Ned leaned down to loosen the neck of the mailbag.

"Every last one."

"Gunna take a while," Ned snorted, rubbing his jaw. "Want me to help you?"

"Thanks, Ned, but I have to look after these myself," Matthew declined. "You know, respecting a girl's confidence."

"Course. Fine," Ned nodded in agreement. "Looks like pretty hard work to me all the same." He finished off the rest of his tea. Good tea, too. Red made a nice cuppa. "Reckon I can stay overnight?" He was hoping Red would say yes, and he did.

"You know you can, Ned." Matthew gathered the few plates together, put them on the tray. "Listen, we're doing a little muster at Yanco Gully. Want to ride along?"

"Count me in!" Ned said with enthusiasm, jumping to his feet. "This Jabiru is a great place. And haven't you made it work!"

Red mightn't want to know it but he had surely inherited Macalister's legendary drive. It was an absolute tragedy when a man rejected his own son, Ned thought. Moreover, *such* a son! And his *only* son. Macalister for all his millions and his empire must have plenty of bad moments.

"I'm serious about this," Julie called as Cassie walked out onto the magnificent upper deck with its breathtaking views of a glorious blue sea and the off-shore islands that adorned it like rings of jade. "That guy's fantastic."

Outside the wind off the water was whipping through Cassie's hair. She hesitated a moment then returned to the huge open-plan living room. "I've told you before, Julie, this is one dangerous-edged man. He won't take kindly to any little jokes. He strikes me as a man with a real temper. He could confront you about it."

"Well—" Julie was seated at a table trying to answer Red's advertisement. "You're not *listening,* sweetie. I'm dead serious. I need some excitement in my life and he's offering."

"You're talking absolute rubbish." Cassie took a chair at the circular table. "And what about Perry?"

"You've got no idea, have you? I said I want *excitement.* Perry's nice, but no one could call him macho. Red is real *man!*"

"And too powerful for you. I wouldn't want to be the woman who tried to make a fool of him. You'd be left with a very sorrowful tale to tell."

"He's not a guy to beat a woman up," Julie scoffed. "He seemed very different from that."

"Well, what do you actually know about him? Zilch."

"I know the best already. I can work my way to the worst. It could just work out." At this Cassie shot out of her seat and Julie fired off, "If you weren't such a control freak you'd admit he got to you, too. I thought that was real sexy the way he kept calling you Cassandra. I wonder what happened to his mother?"

"Something bad," Cassie snapped. "It wasn't a subject he was about to discuss. You did see that."

"Simmer down, Cass," Julie begged. "I'm not clever like you. I want to find myself a *man*. So far, Red's it."

The shrill voice of the vacuum cleaner cut through their conversation. Molly Gannon who with her husband Jim, acted as caretakers for the Maitlands' very expensive retreat appeared from the hallway. "Not going to bother you am I, girls? I can come back later."

"No, come in Molly," Julie beckoned. "You might be able to help us here." Julie turned in her chair. "You know everyone around here. What do you know about a guy called Red Carlyle. Owns a cattle station in the hinterland."

"Red?" Molly switched off the vacuum cleaner and straightened up, pressing a hand against her aching back. "'Course I know Red. Everyone knows Red. He's a big success story around here."

"Ah," Julie cried in satisfaction. "Pull up a chair, Molly."

"Can't we leave this?" Cassie was exasperated and more upset than she knew why.

"It's not Red's ad?" Molly settled herself in an armchair.

"You know about it?" Cassie asked.

Molly gave her rich, rumbling laugh. "We *all* know about it. If I didn't have Jim I'd be applying myself. Mavis at the post office reckons she's flat out handling his mail."

"So they're answering already?" Julie bit her lip.

Molly just looked at her. "You've *seen* Red, haven't you?"

"Yes we have," Cassie told her quietly.

"Talk to him?"

"Just a few words."

"That'd be enough, I reckon." Molly nodded her head. Up and down several times. "He's really somethin', isn't he? He came here with his mum when he was about twelve years old. Wild kid then and for a long time after. A real hot temper. Typical redhead. Used to zip into anyone who said anything about him or his mum. His mum especially. He was very protective."

"What could they possibly *say?*" Cassie asked, somehow fearful of what was coming.

"Aa-ah!" Molly retorted, shaking her head from side to side.

"Come on, Moll," Julie urged. "You can't leave us up in the air. If you want to know, I'm thinking of answering his ad."

"What?" Molly couldn't hide her shock. "You're not *serious* are you, dear?"

"Sure." Julie gave her a challenging look. "I'm real interested."

The odd, shocked expression was still on Molly's face. "Deary, deary, be *warned.*" She gave it such emphasis.

Cassie turned to Julie. "Isn't that what I told you?"

"He hasn't spent time in jail, has he?" Julie demanded, her eyes turning steely.

"No, no, nothing like that." Molly scratched her springy grey head, locking eyes with Cassie, who she thought was far the more sensible of the two. "I said that badly. Red is a fine young man. He's worked very hard to get where he has. We all admire him, but he's got a bit of a cloud over his name. If you know what I mean. Doesn't mean anything to us up here, but it would to *your* folks. Take my advice, girls. Enjoy yourselves and go home. Your life's not up here."

"Is that today's lecture?" Cassie smiled to take the edge off her words. What Molly had said had only made her defensive. On Red's behalf.

"I'm only trying to give you good advice," Molly maintained, now staring at the floor. "Your parents wouldn't thank me, Julie, if I didn't put you straight."

"Why don't you?" Cassie invited. "What's Red's dark secret?"

Molly thought for a moment then sighed. "No *secret* in these parts. He's the flamin' image of his father at the same age, that's why. The colouring. The red setter hair, the blue eyes, the black eyebrows. You've got no idea, have you?"

"Obviously not," Cassie said, and Julie made a snorting sound.

"He's Jock Macalister's son," Molly announced like he was royalty.

Julie sat up, chin up. "For crying out loud!"

"Wait a minute." Cassie frowned. "Sir Jock doesn't have a son. He has three married daughters and as far as I know their children are little girls."

"How come you know so much?" Molly gave her a puzzled stare.

"My parents are quite friendly with Sir Jock," Cassie confided. "They've visited Monaro Downs a number of times. I've been there years ago when I was a child. I don't remember Sir Jock having red hair. It was thick and tawny, as I recall. But I do remember his black eyebrows and brilliant blue eyes."

"He's Macalister's son, all right," Molly said in such a stern voice her double chin trembled. Her disapproval of Macalister was very evident. "Won't acknowledge him though."

Cassie felt heat spread all over her skin. "But that's appalling!"

"It is, too." Molly gave another vigorous sideways jerk of her head. "I can't begin to tell you how that boy suffered. And his mum. The prettiest little thing you ever laid eyes on. Rather like you in style, Julie. Petite, blond. She was English. Posh accent. We all wondered about her background. Red sounds like a Pom to this day."

"But how did they meet?" Cassie asked, clamping her own hands together. "Red's mother and Macalister?"

Molly blew out a long, whinnying breath. "Appears she was employed as a governess, nanny, some such thing, on one of his stations."

"So he took advantage of her?" Cassie said, seeing the tragedy.

"Sure. Don't they all?" Molly retorted caustically, though sadness spread over her kind, homely features. "Little thing was killed a few years back. The whole town turned out for the funeral. Seems like yesterday. It was rough on Red. He really loved his mother. Did everything he could to look after her."

"How was she killed?" Cassie felt a little sick. Julie sat slumped in her chair as though all the wind had been knocked out of her.

"Road accident," Molly said vaguely. "Red's carrying a lot of baggage."

"One can understand that," Cassie mused.

"He'll make a good husband and a good father, mind you," Molly said loyally. "But don't you two young ladies go thinkin' of answering any advertisements. That would rock your folks to the core."

*   *   *

By mutual consent both girls left the house and headed for the beach, walking barefoot in the fine-grained white sand that ran like hot silk.

"Let's move down to the water's edge," Cassie murmured. "Easier going. We'll walk up to Leopard Rock."

The water at the edge was crystal, a beautiful aquamarine that deepened into brilliant blue.

"Well, that sure put a lid on it," Julie groaned. "Poor old Red. It must be awful to be illegitimate."

"It's not the social stigma it once was," Cassie said steadily. "And rightly so. The innocent can't be victimised. They can't pay for something that happened before they were born. Anyway, plenty of couples are having children without getting around to marriage."

Julie nodded, flipping a blond curl out of her eyes. "But it's not *our* way, is it? Our folk's way."

"I guess not. I don't really believe it's any woman's preferred way. Women want security, permanence, the best possible life for their children. There are enough hurdles surely?"

"But what an extraordinary story." Julie bent to pick up a very pretty sea-shell. "Your parents so friendly with Macalister yet they've never heard the rumours?"

"They could have for all I know." Cassie shrugged. "It seems to be common knowledge."

"Yet the family, the Macalisters, ignore it. Ignore Red. He's got a big family with tons of money yet he's an outcast."

They stopped to watch a flock of disturbed seagulls take to the air.

"You haven't met *Lady Macalister*." Cassie shuddered, turning to Julie with a theatrical expression.

"Even my mother said she's a woman with a very cold heart."

Julie would have laughed at the irony if it weren't so sad. "Well, she'd know." She put an arm around Cassie's waist. "Why don't we go and look at this place? Jabiru. It can't do any harm. I'd really like to see it, wouldn't you?"

Of one accord they walked into a foaming little breaker. "Actually I *would* but it'd be against my better judgement. We might be getting drawn into something here, Julie. Something about Red Carlyle scares me."

"Afraid of his attraction?" Julie gave her friend a shrewd glance. "I'd say you're even more interested in Red than I am."

Cassie frowned. "That's the part that bothers me. I can just imagine telling my parents I was interested in Jock Macalister's illegitimate son."

"Can't wait for that one," Julie quipped. "They'd give you a very hard time. Your dad would probably zap you out of his will."

"I don't care about that." Cassie threw back her head, letting the sea breeze whip her hair into a silk pennant. "I've had a good education. I can make my own way. Besides, there's Grandma's money."

"That's right!" Julie brightened. "Tell you what, we'll have a swim on the way back then I'm going up to the house to leave a message for Red. He did invite us and we've got the time. We could take care of his mail for him. Help him pick out the right bride."

In the end Red organised everything himself. He enlisted the help of a friendly neighbour, Bob Lester, a well-established cattleman, to ferry the girls back after his business meeting in town. Red himself would drive them home. But it meant an overnight stay.

"What do you think, Marcy?" Cassie whispered across the counter. They often came into the pub now and each time they had a conversation with a willing Marcy.

"Safe as houses," Marcy maintained stoutly.

"What a pity. I thought he'd grab me," Julie giggled.

"Not Red, I swear. He'll treat you like the fine young ladies you are. Bob and Bonnie Lester are pillars of the community. You'll be safe with Bob. You'll need riding gear. Big shady hats. Red has organised with me to send a few supplies out. You'll take them along on your trip. Bob doesn't mind. I think you're going to have a very good time."

I'll pray for that, Cassie thought.

Bob Lester turned out to be a tall, hale cattleman with a thick shock of prematurely snow-white hair and a full white moustache, handlebars and all. He picked them up at the house and entertained them with lots of stories on their long journey into the hinterland.

Cassie had thought it might be endless but the time flew. The scenery was remarkable. Under a cloudless cobalt-blue sky the countryside waved a lush emerald-green to the horizon. The spurs of the Great Dividing Range stood in stark relief above the plains, their colour the most wonderful moody grape-blue into purple. Small white and lavender-blue wildflowers floated on this sea of hardy green grasses and scattered all over were pools of tranquil water, relics of the floodwaters Cyclone Amy had brought down.

"You can consider yourselves fortunate, girls," Bob Lester told them. "Red don't have many visitors.

He's been pretty darn content on his own. Leastways up until now. I'm blessed if I know if he's serious about this advertisin' for a bride. There's already bagsful of mail arriving from all over. He'd be well advised to be serious, I reckon.''

"So how's he going to handle it?" Julie, in the back, piped up.

"I don't rightly know," Bob admitted. "What I *can* tell you is the woman who lands Red is one mighty lucky woman. Even I never imagined he could work the wonders he has. Jabiru was terribly rundown and the old homestead was in such a state it had to be demolished. Red built the new place with his own hands. It's a credit to him but you'll be able to see for yourselves. Course he's a chi—''

"Chip off the old block?" Julie promoted.

Bob gave a wry grin. "Everyone knows around here. Macalister ignoring his own son. Makes yah wonder!''

"There's no room for doubt?" Cassie asked.

Bob gave her a brief telling look. "None, unless a man has a double.''

It was a paradise of the wild.

Flocks of magpie geese flew overhead and a solitary jabiru stood in stately silence at the edge of a silvery pool. A big sign above the iron gate announced the entry to Jabiru Station. Another sign on the fence carried the warning: This Gate Must Be Shut At All Times.

Cassie jumped out to open the gate, waited until the Land Rover had passed through, then swung the gate back into position. The metallic sound caused an amazing number of brilliantly coloured parrots to rise out of the magnificent gum that stood to one side of the gate, screeching their arrival. Not that Red would have heard. They had to travel a good mile up an unsealed drive before the homestead came into sight. A long, low-slung building that seemed completely at home in its verdant surroundings.

"Say, this is nice," Julie breathed. "But very isolated. He must find it hard out here all by himself."

"Well, he's aiming to change that," Bob said. "Probably he's had no time to feel lonely. He's slaved to get this place back to what it was."

Red was on hand to greet them, all taut and terrific male grace, coming down to the vehicle and opening up the front and back doors. "Right on time!" He looked beyond Cassie for a moment to smile at Bob. "Thanks a lot, neighbour. You'll stay and have a cup of tea?"

"Love to." Bob grinned. "Lots of supplies in the back, Red. Cold stuff in the esky. Marcy sent it along."

"Good. I'll take care of it. You hop out and stretch your legs. Well, now, Julie, Cassandra, I'm very pleased you could come."

The blue eyes made Cassie feel hot and helpless, but Julie answered for both of them. "It's great to be here. Worth working hard for, Red?" She swept out her arms.

"What do *you* think?" Suddenly he turned his head and pinned Cassie's eyes.

For a moment she forgot to breathe. "A paradise of the wild," she managed at last, her voice faintly husky.

"I'll accept that." He smiled. "Come on, come on up. Bob—" he turned his head "—leave those things I'll get them."

"Just the esky, then," Bob answered, reaching into the vehicle for the cold stuffs. "I'll have a cup of tea, then I'll be off."

Inside the bungalow both girls were astonished at how attractive Red had made it. It was rustic, admittedly, the furnishings were old, inexpensive, but comfortable-looking with several sofas, one good leather armchair in a rich burgundy. The scatter rugs on the polished floor were colourful, as were the fat cushions on the sofas. There were prints that looked like they'd been selected carefully, hung around one large main room with a whole wall taken up with books, books, books. Heaps too many to count. There were even two big planters containing luxuriant golden canes and sprays of yellow orchids in a copper pot in the middle of the dark-timbered old dining table that had been polished to quite a shine.

"Come on, a decorator did this," Julie cajoled. "What's her name?"

"This was put together by a man." Cassie looked around. "It's comfortable and relaxed and it has a great feel of home."

"Glad you like it." Red sketched a bow. "While you look around I'll bring your things in. My guest-room is to the left. Two single beds. Clean sheets. I hope you'll be comfortable."

What have I let myself in for? he thought as he lopped down the front steps. The cute little Julie didn't bother him. She was pretty, never giving herself a moment to get bored, but Cassandra of the luminous eyes. He was far from immune to her. In fact for a moment there when they had arrived he had hardly dared to look at her. But still, he had. Stared at her oval face, her skin, her eyes, the luscious tender curves of her mouth, the way her gleaming hair went into deep soft waves over her shoulders.

It was one hell of a risk to have her here, he thought as he reached into the Land Rover for the luggage. Why hadn't he just let it go? Last night when he wasn't cleaning house in preparation for their visit, he had sat reading a score of letters from young women who had given serious consideration to spending their life with him. Some of the letters moved him. Those were from young women from unhappy homes, desperate to find security and a new life. Some of them he even knew. Couple of kooks. One he put down fast. Dirty talk, for God's sake. He realised he might expect it.

Now this beautiful porcelain creature who stood inside the rough house he had built had said it had a great feel of home. She wasn't just saying it, either. He could see the sincerity in her lovely features. The princess he could fall in love with. The princess he couldn't wait to be gone. Jock Macalister's bastard he might be, but he wasn't any fool.

CHAPTER FOUR

BECAUSE Julie couldn't ride, he drove them around the station until late afternoon, stopping to watch the glorious tropical sunset from Warinna Ridge. Fiery reds, glowing rose, brilliant streaks of indigo and gold that illuminated the whole world.

"We'd better not delay," he murmured at last, "dusk will set in fast and we have to get down the ridge." They had left the Jeep at the bottom, making the fairly easy climb on foot. It would be easier still going down. Red went ahead, holding any low-slung branches out of their way, moving with his special rhythm that had Cassie's eyes glued to his wide back.

That was when it happened.

As Julie padded past her just a little out of breath, the ground seemed to move under Cassie's feet. Pebbles and small rocks rolled down the slope. She gave a little shriek as she lost balance, skidding forward, a sharp rock slashing at her ankle as she seemed all set to take a fall. Except it didn't happen that way. Red whipped around in a lightning flash, grabbed her body and hauled her to him, holding her strongly as she fell crushed against him on legs as wobbly as a new born foal's.

"Lord!" she gulped on something that sounded like a sob, her heartbeat driven up into her mouth.

His body was so beautiful. Beautiful! The male scent of him so clean and warm and so erotic. She felt wildly aroused in an instant. Sinking in a well of sensation. And he knew it. He *knew* it. She was more alive than she had ever been. More afraid.

"Cassandra." He bent his head, his mouth touching her hair. "You okay?"

While Julie called out anxiously, "You're not hurt, are you, Cass?"

"I might have hurt my ankle." She spoke breathlessly, betrayingly, feeling the shame of it.

"Here, let's have a look," he said with measured gentleness. "Rest your hand on my shoulder."

She had to get herself under control, glimpsing something wonderful but afraid to follow.

"You've gashed it," he told her. To a man he would have added, "No big deal." But this was a princess with a fine delicate ankle. "Have you got a clean handkerchief on you?"

He gazed up into her face, finding her pale with sexual feelings briefly glimpsed before the veil fell.

"I have." Julie came to the rescue. "Say, that looks nasty, Cass."

"It won't be when I clean it up," Red retorted, fixing a makeshift bandage. "Bad luck. Want me to carry you?" he asked, powerfully aware of his desire to hold her.

Her beautiful hair bounced loose all around her flushed face. "No, I'll be fine." She denied what she longed for. "It just shook me a little."

Understatement of the year. Inside she was burning hot. Imagining herself alone with him in the night. What it would be like?

When they returned to the house, Red insisted on cleaning up the gash straight away.

She protested again, jittery, not knowing what to do

with her hands. She couldn't believe she could feel this way. So soon.

"I think I should. I'm your host. While I'm attending to it, maybe Julie would like to pick the makings for a salad while it's still light?"

"Will do," Julie answered obligingly. "Just so long as you don't ask me to cook the dinner."

"You mean to tell me you can't cook?" He turned on her with sparkling eyes.

"No." Julie grinned. "I guess that means I can't respond to your advertisement."

"Cooking is pretty important. Bottom line." He smiled.

"Where are we going to do this?" Cassie asked as Julie picked up a basket used for the purpose and moved out of the back door to the vegetable garden.

"This way, please." He gestured towards the bathroom which was surprisingly spacious. Built to accommodate a big man, she supposed. Here again, on a limited budget and doing most of it himself, it was bright, attractive with floods of light in the daytime and timber screening. Privacy for guests, she guessed, because there was no one around for miles. There was a long bench in the shower recess and Red told her to sit down there while he hunted up his first-aid kit which lay behind the mirrored wall cabinet.

"This is silly. I can do it." Cassie swept her hair out of her eyes, determined not to let her guard down completely.

"Why so nervous?" His tone was moving them into a new zone.

For a moment she had a dazed, mindless feeling, knowing herself to be transparent. "I think you know the answer."

He stared at her for a moment, a stare as intimate as a kiss. "And what's that?"

Cassie set her delicate jaw, not rejoicing in her vulnerability. "I know you got a lot of mail, Matthew, but don't let it go to your head."

His eyes flickered. "Why not, with a highly desirable woman like you? Anyway, some of these letters would break your heart."

"I suppose." Somehow she wasn't surprised by his sensitivity. "Most of us are looking for something. Someone."

"*You* wouldn't have to look far, would you?" he asked ironically, filling a basin of water and tipping in antiseptic. "I bet you have a string of guys standing in line."

"Well—" A shadow crossed her face. "No one I care about. It takes time to find the right person."

He wanted to touch her cheek, stroke it, run a finger across the lush pad of her mouth. Have that mouth open to him. "And sometimes that person enters your life when you least expect it. The element of chance that can make or break a life. Who said you could call me Matthew?" he asked belatedly on a soft growl.

"It just seemed natural. You don't like it?"

"Maybe too much," he said with a trace of self-derision. Very gently, he removed Julie's blood-stained handkerchief, set it aside, then began to bathe Cassie's ankle. "You have very delicate ankles. Pretty toes." He traced his finger this way and that, slow and steady. Along her instep, over her ankle, down her toes, which she thought gratefully were as nice in their way as her fingers.

"Stop that, Matthew." Her voice was silky soft. Shaky. She knew how much she was giving away.

He paid little attention. "I just thought a little massage." The compulsion to draw her into his arms was becoming unbearable.

"It's not clear to me but, but are you flirting?" Best to sound a little angry.

"Flirting!" He threw back his handsome head and laughed. "Oh, Cassandra, I've never flirted in my life. Never had the time."

"All the same, I think you're dangerous to me."

"You're not going to interfere with my plans, either," he said with a taut smile, picking up the tension.

"If you want to put the bandage on."

"Bandage? Maybe a little Band-Aid?" he lightly mocked, his eyes sliding over her.

"Sure. Make fun of me."

"I'm not like that, Cassie." He held her foot gently and dabbed it dry. "In fact I'm going to kiss it better."

She didn't move. She didn't make a sound. This was seduction itself. Her eyes closed as he bent his glowing ruby head and kissed the smooth skin of her ankle.

"You devil!" she said softly. "No."

"No, what?" He smiled back at her.

"Mocking me again?"

"You know exactly what I'm doing, Cassie." He clipped his words, but his sapphire gaze held her with intensity. "Maybe you'd better make allowances for—"

"A pretty complicated guy?" she suggested, strong emotion leaping from him to her.

"Is that how you see me?" He rose from his haunches and stood up, towering over her, causing her to eye him with trepidation.

"I'm sure of it."

"Why did you come out here?" he challenged very quietly.

She clasped the bench with her two hands, fixing her gaze on the white duckwood floor in the shower. "You invited us. We had nothing else to do. And we genuinely wanted to see the place. Which I must tell you I love."

"For a visit of two days?" he asked cynically.

"What do you want me to say, Matthew?"

His eyes held hidden currents. "Nothing. Heaps. What does it matter?" He looked down at her, his attitude as intense as hers. "How does that feel?"

"Fine." She transferred her gaze to her ankle. "You're very competent in everything you do."

"A top guy."

"You really expect something to come of this advertising?" she burst out spontaneously, revealing part of her turbulent feelings.

"I'm sure something will."

"What about love?" What did it have to do with her, anyway?

"Love can be poisonous, Cassandra. I know that." He looked through and beyond her.

She stood up abruptly, pushing the heavy fall of her hair behind her ear. "You can't let what happened to your mother affect your life."

Too late, she realised her mistake, but she was hopelessly off balance in his presence.

His eyes burned into her like a blue jet of flame. "So the lovely Lady Cassandra has been gossiping?" His expression turned into hard arrogance.

She held up her hands, almost in supplication. "Sorry, Matthew. Please don't call it gossiping. It came out."

"Sure." He shrugged a shoulder. "Who did you ask?"

She could feel the hot blood suffusing her face. "I'd prefer not to say, but someone who's on your side."

"Not Marcy, surely?"

"No, not Marcy. I'm such a fool. I can't believe I blustered that out. But you unnerve me." Just how much she didn't want to fathom.

"If it comes to that, you unnerve me," he said in a grating voice. "So you know the other bit, as well."

She backed away, leaning against the far wall. "Jock Macalister is stuck with his wrong, Matthew. You aren't. You've made a successful life for yourself. You don't have to account to anyone."

There was a voice in the hall. Julie's.

"Hey, you guys, what's happening?"

Red straightened but there was tension in his lean powerful body.

"Coming, Julie," he called in a perfectly calm voice. "I've been attending to Cassandra's ankle."

"Want to tell Red about how I hurt myself skiing?" Julie called. "Boy, that's some vegetable patch, Red. It was hard not to pick the lot."

"Take some home with you tomorrow," Red said, leading Cassie back into the main room. "I'm not the market gardener, by the way. One of my men, Charlie, part Aboriginal, part Chinese in another life, handles that."

"Well, it's a credit to him," Julie said, beaming at them over a basket laden with lettuce, fat red tomatoes, shiny green and red capsicums, shallots and a few lemons she had pulled off a tree. "Say, everything all right here?" Her bright smile faltered after a moment.

"Of course it is," Red assured her so smoothly she

was put at her ease. He held out his hand and took the basket. "The ankle is giving Cassandra a bit of gip."

"Well, sit down girl." Julie hurried over to her. "Take the weight off it. Read a book. Red's got a whole library. Meanwhile he's going to give me a lesson on preparing— What's on the menu, Red?"

"What about peppered steak, Jabiru eye fillet, melt in your mouth. Salad and some little new potatoes. Just dug up. Nice bottle of red. White, if you prefer. Cheese for later. One thing I haven't gotten around to cooking is a cake."

Julie went on in her vivacious fashion. "Then let Cassie show you. She makes a wicked chocolate cake."

Red's two cattle dogs, Dusty and Jason, had returned at sundown and he went out and greeted them affectionately introducing them to the girls but not letting them through the door. They stayed out on the veranda, growling gently in the dark when some movement or sound alerted them.

"They're superb working dogs. Watch dogs, as well," Red said.

In the end they stayed up late, their conversation covering a wide range of topics. Cassie folded herself into the corner of a sofa while Julie took the armchair opposite Red and laughed delightedly at all his stories. And he, like Bob Lester, had a fund of them. In turn she regaled him with funny episodes from hers and Cassie's shared life. Which he appeared to enjoy.

"Now that I've run out of stories," she announced over a nightcap, "what about if we help you to run through a few more of your letters? You'll have to hire a secretary anyway."

"I don't think so, Julie." Red rubbed his forehead,

starting to debate with himself. "Maybe I should. I never expected anything like this, I have to tell you. I won't have the time to get 'round to all of them.

"We'll help you," Julie repeated.

"But they're *personal*," he stressed.

"They won't know."

"That's not the point, is it?" He gave her a wicked smile.

"We'll take the task very seriously, Matthew," Cassie promised. "Assemble the ones with the most appeal."

"All right. All right." A little exasperated, he rose to his six plus, went to a cabinet, selected another twenty letters and slammed them down on the old cedar wood chest he was using for a coffee table. "We won't speak and we won't dare laugh. We'll just set aside what seems to come from the heart. Ah, yes, the photograph, too," he added with humour. "I'm not aiming to ruin my life. I set the limit at thirty."

"The old biological clock, eh?" Julie muttered, selecting one of the pile.

"I want children." Red snatched up one, making short work of opening it out.

And I wouldn't mind mothering them, flashed into Cassie's head.

She woke from a sound sleep for a few moments almost completely disoriented. The clouds of mosquito netting, the narrow bed, the strange room, the incredibly fresh and balmy air that wafted through the windows. Where was she? Then full consciousness set in. She had chosen to visit Matthew Carlyle on Jabiru.

It was early. Very early. The predawn sky was a translucent pearl grey. She slipped her feet out of bed and reached for her robe. Julie, the night owl, was still fast asleep, her two hands tucked sweetly under her chin. Cassie found herself smiling. Julie had slept like that since she'd been a little girl.

Cassie walked to the tall window looking out over the green valley. There was a radiance on the horizon, a radiance that would turn into an explosion of light as the sun burst over the top of the range. Such a beautiful place! It made her feel rejuvenated, more at peace with herself than she had been for a while.

The dawn wind was stroking rustling sighs out of the trees that surrounded the homestead. Gums and acacias, a magnificent poinciana that would be something to see when in flower, numerous bauhinias, the orchid trees and a pair of tulip trees covered with opulent coral-red flowers. From this angle she could see an old tank stand smothered in cerise bougainvillea that cascaded right to the ground. She was truly fascinated by Matthew's world. No wonder he loved it.

Matthew. Matthew Carlyle. Red Carlyle. She tried the names over silently on her tongue. What exactly did he mean to her? How had she reached this stage of involvement—no, "involvement" didn't say it—in such an impossibly short time? True, he was stunningly handsome, bore himself like a prince, was uncommonly well read, highly intelligent. Those attributes hadn't blinded her before. Her ex-boyfriend, Nick Raeburn, with whom she worked, was all of these things as had been a few men before him. What they lacked, or significantly what they lacked for her, was Matthew's brand of magnetism. It penetrated to her very depths. She had been drawn headlong toward him at first sight. Up close and personal he stirred her even more, a combination of the physical and spiritual. He had such *power*.

She was twenty-four. She was moving along in her career, well paid, successful, but something vital was lacking in her life. She thought of it as her dream. To be blessed with the right man. To create a good future together. To love and above all to *share*. Was she crazy to think she could put her needs down on paper? Show them to him. Offer to become his wife.

She wasn't that brave. He would throw back that dark gleaming red head and laugh. A hard ironic laugh. He saw her, she knew, as someone who came from a different world, she didn't dare mention her parents weren't merely acquaintances but friendly with the man who had fathered him only to spend a lifetime ignoring his very existence. Thanks to Jock Macalister, Matthew trusted no one on earth. He wouldn't trust her, either.

Cassie turned away from the window, opened the bedroom door very quietly and listened for sound. Nothing stirred. The dogs weren't on the veranda. She padded down the hallway to the bathroom, found it empty and shut the door. Her towel was there in its allotted place, her bath things. She would have a quick shower and maybe cook breakfast. The truth was Matthew could fend for himself. The steaks last night had been cooked to perfection, the salad, which he'd insisted on making though she'd offered, at its simple best, crisp and fresh tossed in a good olive oil and red wine vinegar.

She was touched by the way he lived. Admired it, too. A man alone, yet keeping everything spick-and-span. He'd allowed her to set the table using an attractive cloth and napkins, good quality dinnerware, stainless-steel cutlery. He was a civilised man with innate good breeding. She wondered what his English mother had been like. A road accident, Molly had said. Leaving a lot more unsaid.

She knew what Matthew's mother looked like. There were several photographs atop an old pine chest in the living room. Photographs of a very pretty blond woman with a bubble of soft curls and a lovely smile, looking unselfconsciously at the camera. Others with her arm around a little boy so handsome he would bring tears to any woman's eyes. Matthew as an older boy, already inches over his mother's head, then an arresting young man, holding his petite mother in front of him, two hands resting on her shoulders. It was evident they were very close.

Cassie was returning very quietly to the bedroom when suddenly a door snapped shut.

Matthew. And no way to avoid him. It brought her close to trembling. Matthew Carlyle, a random element in her life but so compelling it seemed like he was everything she had ever wanted in a man. Cassie stood arrested, the blood coming up into her face.

At that moment Matthew, moving across the living room towards the kitchen, caught sight of Cassie in the hallway.

For a minute he felt like someone had struck him high in the chest. It was a terrible shock to discover he wanted this woman, this near stranger, so very badly. How had this happened? He wanted to touch her, to feel her touch him. She was wearing a blue robe with some sort of lustre, her hair, that wonderful crowning glory, billowing around her shoulders, the outline of her body, sloping shoulders, the small high breasts, delicate hips, just barely concealed by the satiny fabric of her robe.

"Hi there!" he managed when inside he felt hot and heavy, his heart squeezed by emotion. She started to walk towards him as if at a silent call, looking at him with luminous eyes.

She might have been a sleepwalker or someone in a dream so directed was her progress. He found himself putting out a hand, spearing his fingers through the long thick mass of her hair. It came to him he would love to brush it. Have her sit there while he brushed through its deep waves, listening to the electric crackle, revelling in the sable flow over her shoulders.

She should have been startled but she wasn't. She just stood there mesmerised letting him take control.

"How beautiful you are," he said very quietly, lost in the pool of her eyes. "I didn't want you to come, Cassandra," he told her.

"Why?" She knew the answer, her own heart quaking.

"Not difficult to explain. I'm trying to sort out my life, not get in way over my head."

"Of course, I understand that." Still she watched him.

"So why are you looking at me with those river eyes?"

"I thought you *knew*," she said at last.

He nodded. "Sometimes things happen that should never happen." Despite himself his hand moved to her flawless flower skin. His desire for her was growing to the point he knew he should move away, say something about getting breakfast. Anything but pander to his own unparalleled sexual need. Something about her struck such a painful chord. The memory of love. *Real* love. The great love he had had for his mother. The sense of desolation and loss he had endured. His feeling for this woman, Cassandra, was undreamt of. In pursuing it he could cause great unhappiness for them both.

He heard her draw in a little shaken breath and his eyes dropped to her mouth, dwelt on its smooth cushiony curves. Her lips were parted and he could see the pearly nacre of her teeth. Did he imagine it or did she sway towards him? Her long-lashed eyes were wide open, yet so dreamy, so rapt, she might have lost all orientation.

It seemed to work both ways. He found himself taking her oval face in one hand and then he bent his head, caught up her lips with his own, kissing her so deeply, hungrily, it even seemed he was trying to eat her.

The scent of her! The wonderful woman fragrance mixed with the freshness of a lemony soap, and the talcum powder reminding him of a baby.

Quite slowly she wound an arm around his neck like a tendril, knowing what that would do to him. No stopping him now. He pulled her into his arms with a low cry, gathering her tightly against him, ravished by the imprint of her beautiful body on his hard frame. What was happening had never happened to him in the past. He had taken women thankfully with gentleness, glad of their responding pleasure. Now his longing was so harsh he felt the arms that closed around her turn to iron. She was afraid and excited at the same time, he could tell. Her head draped back over his arm as she offered up her mouth, kissing him back, exchanging this almost unbearable rapture. It drove him to half lift her from the ground, desperate not just for kisses but to go all the way. Spread her out on his bed, that beautiful hair fanning around her head.

It was outrageous. He knew that. He barely knew her. She was, after all, a rich girl from the city. A guest in his home. He should be treating her with respect. He had begun to run his hand across her breast, aware of an arousal that matched his own. Now, before another towering wave of heat broke over him, he reeled back, releasing her so abruptly her knees started to buckle and she clutched at him like a child.

"I'm sorry." His breath came out like a bitter gasp. This was fantasy. A dream. Not his rough-and-ready world.

"Wait a moment, Matthew," she answered, very gently, very sweetly. "It was my fault as much as yours."

"So what do we do now? Pretend it didn't happen?"

She saw the high mettled set of his head, the blaze in his eyes. "I'm not the girl you'd pick to marry?"

"You're way out of my league, Cassandra," he said, a nerve beating in his temple.

"How can you possibly say that?" She really meant it. He was the kind of man with the vital force to make a mark in the world. The fact of his birth meant little to her beyond the deep well of sympathy she felt for his abandoned mother and a fatherless child.

"Would you introduce me to Daddy?" he asked in a very crisp, confronting way.

"I'd be happy to." None of the young men her parents had lined up could match Matthew.

"Doesn't it upset you, knowing my background?" He frowned, black brows drawn down.

"It upsets me only in the sense it upsets you," she answered simply. "You're your own man, Matthew. You're an achiever. You can take your place anywhere."

"Sure, I know that," he shrugged, "but it doesn't mean your parents mightn't hate me."

It was possible. Matthew Carlyle was very different. "Matthew, I want to tell you my parents have put me through hell. My father is a very successful, clever, overbearing man. My mother lives a highly social life. That's all she cares about."

"Be that as it may, they wouldn't want their daughter to throw herself away on a guy like me. I know without your telling me they've got someone lined up for you. Someone they're accustomed to. Someone with the same background as themselves. Hell, he's probably already chosen."

She couldn't deny it and it showed on her face.

"You'd have to be totally mad to settle for a small-time cattleman, a beautiful creature like you, to spend your life hidden away in the wilds." He laughed ironically. "Now, what about if you get dressed," he suggested, starting to put distance between them. "I'll make breakfast. Orange juice. Pawpaw. Bacon and eggs."

"You'll make someone a wonderful husband," Cassandra said, suddenly feeling humiliated. Put back on some pedestal. Shut away.

"Good of you to tell me," Matthew said with a suave bow. "All I will admit to is that was the best kiss I've ever had in my life. It's quite possible I'll remember it as an old man."

CHAPTER FIVE

"YOU'RE fascinated by him, aren't you?" Julie said, her pretty face betraying her anxiety.

"No," Cassie denied, adjusting her sunglasses.

"You can't fool me, girl. I've been your best friend for sixteen years." Julie shook her head.

"You sound worried, Julie." They were sitting out on the deck enjoying the earthly paradise that surrounded them.

"I am." Julie reached for the sun cream, rubbing some more on her tanned legs. "I'm not such a fool I can't tell you and Red are wildly attracted to one another. You haven't been the same since we arrived home, even I'm getting out of my depth. I know I started all this, but you must know your parents have their own hopes for you. It has to be someone they approve of, Cassie. Someone who will fit in."

"That's right. Aren't you relieved, then, Matthew wouldn't dream of considering me? He actually told me to my face."

Julie laughed nervously. "He *did?*"

"Meeting Matthew Carlyle was like having an abyss open up in front of me," Cassie said.

"Lord, Cassie." Julie sighed deeply. "Not that I can blame you. Red is just amazing. Bright, breezy, arrogant, fun. In truth, quite a guy. I could have fallen in love with him myself but it was perfectly plain he had no interest in me. It was you who caught his gaze that first day on the highway. I can't think why when

I'm far more beautiful.'' She laughed softly then sobered. ''I'm sorry, Cassie. I could have spared you the heartache. You're usually so sensible.'' She shook her head again.

''You think it's a disaster to allow myself to fall in love with Matthew.''

''Oh, boy. *Yes!* I know you've shown plenty of spirit but in a way you're still a mite afraid of your parents. Your father especially. Goodness knows he's a regular despot though he's been a little more human of late.''

''Well, that's because he thinks finally I'm going to toe the line.''

''In a sense my own parents aren't that different,'' Julie admitted. ''They'll want a say in my marriage. That's the only way, according to Mum, I'll get the perfect match. I'm still a kid in the classroom to her.''

''You poor thing! Anyway, it was quite an experience. I'm none the worse for it.''

''You must excuse me if I don't believe that,'' Julie burst out. ''Red's the one person I've ever seen get to you. It would have to be someone totally unsuitable.''

''Ah, yes—'' Now the about-face. ''I've thought a lot about it,'' Cassie said. ''I'm going to answer Matthew's advertisement.''

Horror and a kind of admiration broke over Julie's pretty face. ''But he'll think you're trying to make a fool of him. Heck, Cassie, didn't you warn me not to think of upsetting Red?''

''I'm dead serious.''

This affected Julie so much she jumped up and went to the balustrade, looking out sightlessly over the glorious blue sea. Finally she turned with a sympathetic frown. "There *is* such a thing as love at first sight obviously."

"The poets say so." Cassie had a clear picture of Matthew's face. "I just didn't think it could happen to me."

"Usually I'm the mad, impulsive one," Julie moaned, "and you're so calm and controlled." She came back, dropped a kiss on the top of Cassie's head, then sat down. "This is like a romance novel. It can't be real. Do you realise your parents would blame *me?*"

"Well, I'll tell them you advised me against anything so crazy."

"A wise move for me." Julie sounded wry. "What is it you want, Cassie?" she asked. "Adventure, a rip-roaring life? Can't you have a good old time? Get Red out of your system."

"I want him," Cassie said very carefully.

"Then it's not just sex?" Julie looked hard at her.

Cassie drew off her sunglasses. "We didn't get into that, Julie."

"Oh, yeah, no time?"

"Surprise, surprise. Matthew goes a long way towards being a very chivalrous guy."

Julie shrugged. "I find myself agreeing. You can see his mother's story has affected him deeply."

"Sad but no bad thing," Cassie said with a slight hardening of her tone. "We've both met guys with a callous hand for all their so-called eligibility."

"You're absolutely right. But I should stop you," Julie said.

"Sorry, kiddo," Cassie answered staring up at the sky. "Too much time has passed. I've already written the letter. In fact Matthew should have it by tomorrow.''

The morning had barely dawned before Julie took a call from her mother telling her of the sudden death of her great-aunt.

"You don't have to come with me," Julie said, seeing the torn expression on Cassie's face. "Aunt Sarah lived a good life. At some point in her eighties she decided she didn't want to go on. All the family knew it. I'll have to go to the funeral, show my respects, but you can stay on. We still have to the end of the week.''

"But your parents will expect me to come home with you," Cassie said.

"Not in the least. They're very happy to have you enjoy this. Molly and Jim are here to look after you.''

"We both know the reason why I want to stay, Julie." Cassie met her friend's eyes.

"It might come to nothing, Cassie," Julie warned. "You said yourself Red is one complex man.''

"I know, but I have to hear what he has to say.''

"It could be painful," Julie stressed, "and I won't be here to offer comfort.''

"He could simply ignore me," Cassie said as calmly as she could.

"I don't think that's possible." Julie's answer was wry. "Different backgrounds or not, you both seem to *identify*. It's more than chemistry, I can see that. Just as I can see it might involve a lot of trauma.''

Cassie sipped at her coffee meditatively. "I think I know, Julie, who I am and what I want. I've been drifting unsatisfied, unfulfilled. We've talked about it often enough. I want commitment. A mature relationship before I'm too much older. I want children. I want to share all the pleasure and the pains of my life. I want a husband to love. I want to be able to tell him I love him. I could never say it to my mother and father. Maybe that's one of the reasons I'm drawn to Matthew. I know he wants commitment, too. Family. The stable relationship he never had in his childhood.''

''I know, and it's just beautiful,'' Julie all but wailed, ''but your parents will kill you when they find out.''

Two hours later Julie was on her flight to Sydney, pretty flustered by all that was happening, but vowing not to say anything at all about Cassie's reason for staying on. ''You'll ring me just as soon as you get Red's response.'' She gave Cassie instructions. ''I'm really desperate to know how this turns out. This is your *life*, Cassie. Your future. I thought you were the one who had wisdom.''

Cassie didn't protest. ''I have to pin my faith on my deepest intuitions, Julie.'' She kissed her friend on the cheek and walked her to the departure gate. ''There are no guarantees in life. I've only known Matthew a very short time but I feel in my bones he's a fine human being.''

The same fine human being arrived on Cassie's doorstep late afternoon, eyes flashing blue fire under a fine head of steam.

''What's this supposed to mean?'' he demanded of Cassie without preamble, waving her letter in the air.

''Are you going to come in?'' she invited.

''No, I'm not,'' he returned bluntly. ''How do I know Julie isn't in this with you? Two cruel little city cats having a bit of fun.''

''It's not like that at all, Matthew. No way. I promise. Anyway, Julie has gone home. I drove her to the airport this morning. A member of her family died suddenly.''

"That's awful." His anger dimmed briefly. "I'm sorry. Death hits even the rich. In the meantime, you're staying on. What are you hoping for? An outback adventure. Some fantastic sex?''

She almost laughed then, sobering quickly, said, "No!"

"Come on, Cassandra. I'm a realist. You're playing a game. Well, I'll tell you, lady, with the *wrong* man.''

There were heavy footsteps in the hall. The next moment Molly hove into sight, carrying a huge vase of tropical lilies she had picked that morning. "Cassie, I thought I heard you talking to someone," she exclaimed. Then, when Cassie moved, "Ah, Red, how nice to see you. What brings you to town?''

"Business, Molly." He managed to sound casual. "How did Jim get on on his fishing trip with Deputy Dan?''

"Hear about that, did you?" Molly smiled broadly. "There's nobody knows more about what's goin' on than Red," she told Cassie, placing the spectacular floral arrangement on the circular table. "Don't know how he does it so far out of town.''

"You'd be surprised, Molly, who drops by.''

"The girls certainly enjoyed themselves," Molly stood back to admire her handiwork. "Had a lovely time. I suppose Cassie's told you Julie had to fly off home.''

"Well, yes, but I've just arrived.''

"Come in and have a cup of coffee, then," Molly invited. "Expect you're staying overnight at the pub?''

He nodded. "I'll start back before dawn."

"So, are you comin' in or what?" Molly looked from one to the other, her broad smile fading as she picked up on the atmosphere.

This time Matthew shook his head. "No thanks, Molly. I have a problem to address."

Molly moved uncomfortably. "Oh, sure, right."

"Don't mean to be rude, Moll. I was hoping Cassandra, here, would come back into town with me. We have something to discuss."

"A date, is that it?" Molly asked cautiously.

"Not at all. A *discussion*," Matthew said impassively. "Coming, Cassandra?" He transferred his hard gaze to Cassie's face. Her beautifully sculpted cheekbones were tinged with colour, but her eyes were calm and level.

"If you wait just a moment I'll grab a shirt." Some sort of cover-up. She was wearing a sleeveless indigo top with matching drawstring trousers, but it felt right to put something over the top. For one thing, she wasn't wearing a bra. Matthew's gaze was like a lick of flame.

Molly was staring at them both with a hint of puzzlement. "Everything okay with you two?"

Red flashed her his beautiful smile. "I promise I'll bring Cassandra back safe and sound."

Inside Matthew's Jeep all was quiet but for the knocking of Cassie's heart. Matthew was silent driving on down the coast road, stopping at a point where the beach became accessible.

"Let's go for a walk," he said in a clipped voice, putting the vehicle into park and switching off the ignition.

"All right." She opened out her door and sprang onto the grassy verge.

Everywhere was radiant light, the cobalt-blue sea stretched to the horizon, floating coral cays and emerald islands surrounded by blazing white sand. The throbbing heat of midday had cooled off and the breeze swished through the tall coconut palms and the dense vegetation that gave life and colour to the cascading slopes. Armies of little wildflowers in scarlet, vermilion, deep blue, and gold embroidered the foliage while all about an array of bougainvillea blossomed prolifically.

It was ravishingly beautiful, tranquil, the golden sand shifting beneath Cassie's feet. The water near the edge was so crystal clear she could see all the pretty little shells lying on the seabed. She turned her head, seeing the long stretch of beach to the headland was deserted. There was no one around but the flocks of gulls that took to the air at her unexpected appearance.

Matthew, vigorously crunching his way across the sand, caught up with her and took hold of her arm. She was forced to stop.

"What do you expect to come of all this?"

Her breath caught in her throat at the severity of his expression. She remembered then the stories about his temper.

"Is it so incredible to believe I meant it?" She spoke, emotionally seduced by his gaze. "After all, you've had dozens of letters."

"Dear God." He turned his handsome head towards the sea where a shoal of small fish were leaping from the waves. "I want the truth, Cassandra," he gritted.

"I meant every word." She gave a choked little cry and tried to break away.

He held her hard. "Sorry. I'm not buying it. I suppose the two of you laughed yourselves sick at your boldness."

"Did you think my letter bold?" A stab of deepest anxiety pierced her. She had tried so hard to get it right.

"It would have been a beautiful letter. From a stranger. Not from *you*." He stood proudly, unsmilingly, cleft chin upthrust.

"That's it? Not from *me*." Her spirits lifted. *A beautiful letter*. "I'm like you, Matthew. I want a life. I want a husband, family. I'm longing to live my dream."

"So you said in your letter," he cut her off. "The brutal fact is, you'd hate every moment of living Outback. Even the town is only a very small community. There aren't any theatres, nightclubs, concert halls. No flash department stores and boutiques to go shopping. No luxury. Only peace and quiet and the land."

"You don't think I feel its tremendous attraction?" She looked at him, challenging him to deny it.

"I feel you and I have something utterly different going," he said with hard meaning.

Cassie bent her head in acknowledgment. "I only know I've never felt like this before."

His hands took her shoulders. "How do I know you're not some consummate actress? Why don't you level with me? What do you want, a quick affair before you vanish?"

She blushed. "Do you intend to talk to all the other women who wrote to you like this?"

He ignored her. "Hell, don't you realise you could have been taking a big risk?"

"I trust you, Matthew," she said, and she really did.

Something flashed in his eyes and he grasped the long fall of her hair with one hand.

"What sort of a future could *we* have?"

"A good one if we work at it. I'm not so very different from you. In my own way I was abandoned. That's not going to happen to my children."

He reflected on this with a daunting frown. "You're dreaming," he said at last. "Fantasising. All on the basis of one kiss." Even then there was residual passion in his voice.

"You felt what I felt," she returned simply. "You can't deny it."

"So? It's only because you're so beautiful." He spoke coolly. "A magnolia who shouldn't be uprooted. You don't know anything about loneliness or isolation. Doing it hard. This idea about living happily ever after isn't enough. It takes much more than sexual fascination to make a marriage. Or is it like I said, you're just plain bored?"

It seemed to her she might never convince him. "The first moment I saw you I sensed some part of what was going to happen," she offered.

"Are you going to call it Fate?" His voice was tight.

"Is that so strange?"

"Don't you dare cry," he said sharply, uncertainly.

"It's the salt air in my eyes." She blinked and her voice began to falter. "I promise you, Matthew, my letter was written in all sincerity. I know how you might think it was some kind of a joke. I know I'm as much a mystery to you as you are to me, but I'm not like that. Cruelty, insensitivity, is something I've had turned on me most of my life. The more I see of you, the more I want to learn.''

"This is so damned crazy,'' he muttered in a low voice. "Dangerous. Aren't you scared?''

"Of course I am.'' She spoke nervously. In reality she was intoxicated, out of balance. It was wonderful just to be with him again. Even if he was angry. He was like some marvellous ray of attraction with his intensely male sexuality, his power and vigour, the eyes of a visionary. Who needed safety?

The sky above them began to fill with long billowing clouds to set the sun to rest. Broad golden beams of sunlight were pervaded by a pink mist. Sunset was approaching to silence them with its beauty.

"You know nothing about me, nothing at all.'' He raised a hand to his temple, a gesture of uncertainty, exasperation.

"Some things we take on faith without *knowing* it.'' Cassie was disturbed by her own headlong behaviour.

"You want to escape. You're not happy.''

"I haven't been happy for a while now,'' she said after some moments, staring up at the splendour of the sky.

"I'm surprised to hear that. You're beautiful, rich. Ah, I get it, you've had an unhappy love affair.'' His tone was dry. "You're trying to forget.''

"I don't give a damn about anyone.'' She faced him, catching at her skeining hair. "There is no one. Do you want a wife or not, Matthew?'' she challenged.

"Stop it. Damn it, Cassandra,'' he said as though she was making him feel desperate and trapped. "You're not the right girl to come into my life. You don't understand what you're letting yourself in for.''

"So, I'm rejected?" She felt a weight of terrible dismay.

"Listen, why don't we go into town?" His eyes creased against the setting sun. A glory of crimson rose-pink and gold. "Have something to eat."

She hated herself for agreeing. Tormented now by her vulnerability to the man. "All right," she replied almost curtly.

"I'm sorry, Cassandra, if I don't respond to the shots as you call them."

"I'll keep trying."

"Why would you? Why *should* you?"

"Because it's important," Cassie said with surprising conviction.

By mutual accord they sought something more private than Marcy's, choosing Francesco's, an excellent small restaurant run by a local family with strong Italian roots. Arriving early as they did, the place was almost empty, but as they took their time over a pre-dinner drink other customers began to arrive, some with children, their voices bright and cheerful as they greeted their host and different members of the family, all accomplished cooks, who took turns manning the restaurant. Cassie felt too intense to be hungry but delicious aromas kept wafting from the kitchen whenever the swinging doors opened and shut.

"The ravioli here is wonderful," Matthew mentioned, himself infected by her mood. His face uplit by the blossoming candlelight was all planes and angles. "A simple enough dish yet plenty get it wrong. Frank uses the finest, freshest ingredients. They speak for themselves. Come to think of it, I've never been here when the food wasn't good. We'll eat whenever you're ready, Cassandra. Maybe after that you'll be ready to talk.''

Cassie laughed wryly. Not a terribly good beginning, she thought, but from the first bite of a beautifully tender pillow of pasta with a delectable filling of eggplant and a marvellous sauce which turned out to be melted zucchini flowers, Cassie began to unwind. If only there was no…issue between them, this would be a joy.

Matthew ordered a bottle of red wine and for the space of the meal, which included the classic *vitello tonnato,* they simply savoured the food. Francesco came over to the table smiling broadly, complimenting Cassie on her beauty while they in turn complimented him on a memorable meal.

"How have I never seen you before?" Francesco asked Cassie with a wide grin which embraced Matthew.

"This is my first time." Cassie smiled. "I sincerely hope it won't be the last."

"Not the first time for Red." Francesco clapped hand on Matthew's shoulder. "But the first time I see such a light in his eyes!"

"Hell, Italians are such romantics," Matthew said in a throw-away voice after Francesco had moved on. "I can see what the candlelight is doing to your face, let alone my eyes."

"What is it doing?" Cassie looked at him, her wineglass cupped like a chalice between her two slender hands.

He didn't answer for a moment. "Your skin has turned to pale gold," he began. "Your eyes are no longer silver-grey, they've taken on the violet of your shirt. Your mouth is as tender as a child's but very much a woman's. You're powerfully beautiful, Cassandra. I don't know how to describe what you've got. On the one hand it's all sensuality and plenty of it, on the other, there's high intelligence, a flame of purity, goodness, sensitivity. It's enormously intriguing. Tell me about your childhood.'' He gave her a straight, interested look.

It touched her that he didn't just consider her a body. She sipped at her wine then put it down. "Not uncommon, Matthew.'' When goodness knows it was. "As I've told you, my father is a very successful businessman. Making money is his life. My mother, in her own way, is devoted to him. He provides her with just the sort of life she craves. They travel a great deal. My father never embarks on a business trip without my mother. Their marriage works for them. It's solid.''

"So, material success and high social position are at the heart of it?''

"Very much so,'' she said softly, like a sigh. "A great many people feel that way.''

"You seem a little traumatised by it all.'' He reached across the table, unexpectedly putting a hand over her own, a gesture that made tears sting her eyes.

"I probably was when I was very young. I was a sort of formless little kid. I didn't quite know what my place was in the scheme of things. I wasn't the light of my parents' eyes. I couldn't fail to know that even if I didn't understand it. I had a nanny from birth until I was seven. I loved her and I continue to see her. Then when she left, I was sent off to boarding school. It was there I met Julie. We looked into one another's eyes and were friends. Just like that. Julie's a lot of fun.''

"Yet on the face of it, you don't seem to have a lot in common?" He said it as he saw it, from his own observation.

"Actually we share a great deal of affection and loyalty. Opposites attract." She gave him a slight mocking smile. "Maybe being opposites is essential to balance. You have a dark side to *you*, Matthew."

He nodded his red head. "So I have. We've both lived our little dramas. You seem to have found out about mine." This with a tinge of bitterness.

"It wasn't simple curiosity." She held his gaze. "I wanted to see into your heart and your mind and your soul."

The muscle along his taut jawline worked. "How in earth did it happen?" He ran his fingertips across his wide brow.

"You mean, our attraction? It's not just me, is it, Matthew?"

His handsome face was so still it looked carved. She didn't move, either, waiting on his reply.

"On the basis of one kiss? A couple of days together? Showing you all Jabiru has to offer?"

"It's possible." In the soft warmth she felt a little chill. "I believe there is a connection between events no matter how seemingly random. I don't remember you being so hard on the writers of your other letters."

Still he said, "With a couple of exceptions, they weren't trying to make an ass of me."

Her quick flush answered him. "You know I'm not."

The hardness inside of him softened at her expression. "All right, I accept that, but I have this troubled feeling about it, Cassandra." He looked at her levelly with his piercing eyes.

"You know what it is?" She felt the two of them were locked in a bubble. "You're scared of loving someone, Matthew, and you're trying to protect yourself. You want a woman who'll accommodate all your needs but won't get under your skin. Really falling in love hurts."

A harsh protest rose in his throat. "Not only that, it can muck up a life." He turned his head, looking for a waiter. "Let's have a coffee."

"I don't mind." She lifted the heavy fall of her hair at the back of her neck. The restaurant was entirely filled now, people around them exclaiming at the food, the children tucking into thick crusty bread, mopping up the remains of spaghetti.

"And you'd have to give up your very comfortable life in Sydney, your very good job, the prospects of promotion Julie was talking about, to settle down on an Outback cattle station?" Matthew said eventually. He stopped talking as the waiter arrived with their short black espresso coffees, then left.

"I don't know all that's coming, Matthew," she conceded. "How could I? I thought I wanted a career. It seemed to be important to be a success as my father expected. And I am. I'm well regarded in the firm. But I wouldn't give my life to a career. I told you what I want. Love. Family. Husband, wife, children. The full traditional bit. I've given a lot of thought to this. I've enjoyed the adrenaline rush of my job, the rock beat of big business, getting all the calculations right, but it's not the full picture. The *right* picture. I could love you if you let me. I could love your way of life. I want to share your vision. I admire you so for all you've achieved."

"Have you ever been in love?" he suddenly shot at her. "Tell me *now* before you have time to think."

"No." She paused.

"Is that the truth?"

She looked up at his handsome face and found it taut and hawkish. "Once I thought I was."

"Thank you," he said dryly, his handsome mouth twisting.

"The feeling didn't last."

"So where is he now?" The brilliant eyes stared into her face.

"Actually, I work with him," Cassie admitted, wondering if she should have told a white lie.

"So in a way it *is* flight?" A little cloud of hostility had set in, breaking up the fragile rapport.

She shook her head and said in a neutral tone, which was actually a quiet challenge, "I've no more argument to present, Matthew. I can see your unease. We've only had this short time together, I know, but either you accept me or push me out of your life forever. I have to go home Friday." Either way I've been burnt badly.

"You started this, Cassandra." The words burst from Matthew with the force of pent-up passion. "Now we both have to live with it. I'm damned well not going to give you an instant answer. I know what it's like running around with a ring through the nose. I'm a cattleman remember?"

Francesco came to see them off, exclaiming again at Cassie's beauty, bowing over her hand, giving Matthew another thump on the shoulder, making it look like happy, earthy congratulations. Matthew thought it was time to get out before Frank started

teasing him unmercifully. He and Adelina, Frank's
wife, were always encouraging him to get married.

"Get someone to wait on *you*," Frank often said,
and laughed. "No good, a man being on his own."

He could run off with a beautiful princess. Be totally enraptured until the princess decided she'd had
enough of the back blocks and left him sick of heart
and forsaken. Both of them lapsed into a silence while
he drove back to the luxury hideaway on the headland.

"I haven't asked you what Julie thinks of all this,"
Matthew said finally into the fraught silence.

She didn't turn her face to him. "She's concerned."

"Well, hell, she isn't a fool, exactly."

Her own anger surfaced. "Let it alone, Matthew. I
hear you loud and clear."

"Meanwhile we lust after each other." That when
the beginnings of love were flowing into him and with
it a lot of unexpected stress.

It must have hurt her because she dropped her head,
giving a little smothered cry to which he responded
powerfully.

He braked and scanned the road he knew so well.
A minute later he turned the Jeep off the road, pulling
into a scenic vista bordered by white timber rails. The
sea was shining all around them, the sky fantastic, glittering with stars, the air smelling so sweetly of the sea
and the thousands of little wildflowers that rioted
across the vegetation and down the sandy slopes.

"Ah, Cassie." Beyond composure, finding himself
with her in the melting dark, he moved to clasp her
face between his hands, feeling the trembling that
broke over her as he lowered his head.

She had no standard by which to measure his enormous fascination. It was enchantment, emotion run-

ning so deep she could feel the heat of it on their skin. There was a buzzing in her ears, in her veins. She wanted him with all her body. Very nearly so with all her heart. But she knew he was a lot tougher than she could ever be. She knew he was a man who could make hard decisions. Who would do anything to arrange his life.

His hands moved to her shoulders and stopped there. The bones so delicate, so elegant, he felt steam was actually coming off him, his desire for her was so powerful, burning him up. She wasn't wearing a bra. How could he not notice? That pretty little top all that was between her and her bare skin. The filmy shirt that changed the colour of her eyes fell back like a shawl so all evening he could see the tender, shadowed cleavage, imagining the rose-pink of the nipples that peaked so erotically against the indigo-blue fabric.

The beauty of the night, the scents and the burning diamond-white of the stars were increasing his feelings of wildness, of going out of control.

It shouldn't be. He had worked hard at being his own master. He wasn't going to let go of it for a woman. She was right. It scared him. This feeling of being spellbound like she had stolen his soul.

Her eyes were closed. He knew there were tears behind her eyelids. He kissed them, staring down into her beautiful, luminous face. Was this the woman to take to the rough bush? She deserved the finest mansion. A man who had no stain on his background, not Jock Macalister's bastard son. He thought he had risen above it. Now, with this woman, it was a source of exquisite pain.

"I want you," he groaned. He thought he had his life in near perfect order. How things had changed! He tried to pull her closer but the console was the stumbling block. A tiny barrier yet it seemed insupportable. "We have to get out," he said very urgently, feeling the fine tremble in his hands.

"Hold on." She shook her head frantically, trying to whip herself back to some sort of control. "What *is* it you want of me, Matthew?" she pleaded. This man in some ways was as wild as a falcon.

He let out a shuddering breath. "You haunt me too much. I want to make love to you. Can't you just accept it?"

"No." If she did she would never be free of him. Her body began to arch and she held up her hands defensively. "I've been trying to convince you I could make you a good *wife* and you've been pushing me away. You refuse to take me seriously. You're a man who likes to keep control. I'm too—what do you say?—*exotic* to take a place in your life, but I'm plenty good enough to make love to."

"My God! You are," he rasped. "Actually, Cassandra, you're a first for me."

"You could tell me what that means. A first? You're not taken with the idea? Does it disempower you," she taunted.

Abruptly he reached out and gripped her shoulders. "Already you've got the power to wound." He sobered up at her small cry, softened his grip, apologised. "I didn't hurt you?"

"No." Her head fell forward with a mixture of helplessness and yearning. "There's nothing safe about us. *Nothing.*"

"Not from where I'm sitting." His voice was laced with self-derision. "There's no insurance we can take out."

Now she felt his hand on her long hair, fisting it, drawing it away from her face.

"Matthew." She began trembling, her hair spilling everywhere like silk, but already his mouth came back to hers, so passionate, so sizzling, she could feel her whole system turn molten, then…melt. He was willing her to risk everything, to move down to the beach, allow his hands and his mouth to race over her, her life's blood beating hot and wild beneath her skin. So easy to get her out of her clothes, so light, so fine. He was already slipping her voile shirt and her camisole top from her shoulder, baring it to his mouth that nevertheless spoke a kind of silent love.

"Matthew," she began again before things got totally out of hand.

"I'm so glad you call me that. I thought I would be Red for the rest of my days." He pressed his mouth into the hollow above her collarbone. "Damn you for making a fool of me, glorious Cassandra. Damn you for coming here looking like a princess on a royal visit."

"I really didn't have much say in it," she whispered. "It was Fate."

"So we don't know what we're up against? This could pass for you, Cassandra." He released her edgily and sat back in his seat. "Like a bout of fever. Once you're back in the city among your own kind. Not the least of it the guy in the office who's in love with you. I bet he considers himself among the high fliers. You could talk it over with Julie. Blame it on the tropics."

"That's absolutely wrong." She protested with her first real despair. Didn't he know she couldn't think of anything else *but* him? She drew away trying to straighten her shirt. "Maybe you should stick with a sweet little hardworking country girl, after all. A good cook with a green thumb. One who won't let it bother her you don't really love her. That's life. She answered an advertisement. She's not about to complain. There'll be babies, a home, financial security. She knows how to count her blessings.''

He nodded, indolently, looking unbelievably handsome and thoroughly arrogant. ''Well, hell, Cassie,'' he drawled. ''Any man in his right mind wants a peaceful life, not a woman who befuddles his brain and gets between his ribs and his heart. 'Course I didn't stay long at school. Never went to university. No money for that. We were very very poor. How's that for Jock Macalister's only son?''

Cassie shivered at the bitterness. All the deeply entrenched pain.

''Of course, he's the *only* one who's not certain of who I am,'' Matthew added.

''He'd know it in two seconds if he ever laid eyes on you,'' Cassie burst out, and wished more than anything she hadn't.

''That's a damn odd thing to say, Cassandra.'' He placed a finger under her chin and turned her face to him. ''Explain.''

''I told you. I met him once.''

''When you were a child?'' He raised his distinctive black brows. Macalister's brows.

''I was clever even then. Very observant.''

Still cupping her face with one hand, he ran a very shivery finger behind her silky ear.

''You wouldn't be lying by any chance?''

''No way,'' she said, colouring, glad of the glimmering dark.

''He could very well do business with your company," Matthew continued suspiciously. "He's into everything. Real estate. Freight, oil, energy."

"I met him once in my life." Cassie told the truth, still lacking the courage to reveal the rest. The scent of danger was all around the Macalister name. "I told Molly I wouldn't be out long." She turned her face away, perturbed by her own passion and her slight control. "Why don't you drive me home?"

"I guess that's best." What he felt for this woman was almost against his will, but still he asked, "And our unfinished business?"

"Sleep on it, Matthew," Cassie advised. "Weigh it up."

CHAPTER SIX

HE DIDN'T contact her at all before she went home, knowing it was cruel; just as sure it was necessary. He wasn't quite ready to make the most important decision of his life realising his attitude was coloured by his own early sufferings.

Yet the thought, *What have I done?* raged constantly through his mind. For the first time he found it difficult to sleep, his work-weary body twitching in bed, often until dawn when the soft grey light streamed into his room and he got up to stare out the window. Even the sky reminded him of a pair of luminous eyes.

She would have made the journey back to Sydney thinking him a callous brute. This gave him tremendous concerns. If he was so disturbed, so, he was sure, was she.

But she had to return to her own life, friends and family, her own community, to view what had happened with any detachment. Everyone had heard of a holiday romance. People going on boat trips, having a fling. Flings weren't his nature. He'd had an eternity to ponder on what had happened to his mother. An eternity of bearing the brunt of a rash, ill-advised liaison. It was entirely conceivable once back among her own kind, Cassandra would come to believe their headlong attraction, so wildly at variance with their normal behaviour was just some powerful aberration to be put right. But then, a man of action, he had to *do* something.

It came to him during the night, so the next morning he rose early, got the men together, allocated them their respective jobs then organised a trip to Sydney. Maybe Cassandra wouldn't be thrilled to see him. Maybe she'd refuse to see him. It had been all of three weeks but he had learned something as frightening as it was thrilling. Right or wrong, he didn't want to live without her. She filled him with passion, with energy, a longing to carve out a great future. He knew he had it in him to give her a fine life.

Back in Sydney, Cassie had two priorities. To forget Matthew Carlyle. To keep her mind on her job. She was up for promotion. Julie's father waxed lyrical about her capacity for cutting to essentials, her coolness in tight situations. It was early days, she was a bit young for it, but she was a serious contender for Phil McKinnon's job now that he was moving up in management.

Cassie spent many long hours at her desk, tapping away at her computer, threading her way through innumerable facts and figures. All to prove her prowess. She was very good at tracking and cross-tracking numbers. It was a language she had got to know and understand. She didn't fare anywhere as well trying to forget Matthew. He smiled at her from behind her eyes.

Julie was shocked but relieved at her return.

"Obviously he was deeply attracted to you but he must have realised, Cassie, it would never have worked," she pointed out gently.

"Who the heck knows what is or isn't going to

work?'' Cassie fired back, upset and exasperated. ''There couldn't be an institution more subject to risk than marriage. Falling in love and getting married isn't a guarantee of bliss. It's like being infected by a fever. Neither person can run out and buy insurance.''

''I know. I know, but couldn't you love Nick?'' Julie pleaded. ''He worships the ground you walk upon. Even your father spent quite a deal of time talking to him at our Christmas party, don't you remember?''

Cassie made a dismissive gesture with her hand. ''Nick has mastered the knack of buttering up to V.I.P.'s.''

''True,'' Julie agreed with a wry grimace. ''But he was especially nice to your father for a reason. He's hoping to be looked on as a prospective son-in-law.''

''But it's over, Julie, and it can't be resurrected,'' Cassie said. ''It's Matthew who's captured my heart.''

A kind of despair settled on Julie's face. ''But he was always a wild card, Cass. And he has a very problematic background. What a fight you would have trying to get your parents to accept him.''

''Don't I know it.'' Cassie felt the old familiar knots in her stomach.

''Don't think my heart doesn't bleed for you,'' Julie said quietly, ''but the connection between your father and Red's. Did you ever tell him the *full* story?''

Anxiety seethed in Cassie's soul. ''I regret to say, no. I wanted to, but I couldn't. Matthew would have exploded if I'd said Jock Macalister was my father's *friend* as well as sometimes business associate. Anyway, what does it matter now?'' She sighed and picked up the phone to ring a client. ''Matthew completely rejected me.''

"I could kill him," Julie muttered darkly, seeing Cassie's deep hurt.

"That's okay." Cassie looked at her friend with shadowed eyes. "Given time, I'll get over it."

Cassie had dinner with her parents on the Saturday night, asking Nick along for company, because these supposedly quiet family dinners usually turned into a gathering.

Fourteen in all sat around the gleaming mahogany table, elaborately decked out with the finest china, crystal, silver, exquisite white linen and lace place mats with matching napkins. There were two low crystal bowls of white lilies flanking a filigree silver basket of luscious summer fruits and table grapes. Tapering candles in Georgian sterling silver candlesticks were placed meticulously down the table length.

The overhead chandelier was on the dimmer and candlelight threw a flattering light over the faces of the women. Everyone, with the exception of Cassie, was middle-aged but beautifully preserved through a strict diet and beauty routine. Cassie's own mother, in deep burgundy silk, could have passed for ten years younger, or as Nick put it outrageously on arrival, "I have to hand it to you, Mrs. Stirling. You look more like Cassie's sister with every passing day."

So what does that make me now? Cassie thought wryly. I must be showing the strain. In fact she looked beautiful in white silk crepe scattered with sequins, her mane of hair drawn into an elegant chignon and secured with a bejewelled clip the way her parents liked it. These dinners were invariably black tie. No backyard barbeques for the Stirlings. Her mother, in fact, would not have been caught dead in a pair of jeans.

Now Cassie looked down the table at her father, scrutinising him over the waxy petals of the lilies. He had a wonderful profile, his handsome head turned as he tossed off a joke to one of the women guests. He was a big man. Tall with broad shoulders but not heavy. He looked what he was: a rich, influential man, his personal wealth understated, not commented on.

He really needed a son to carry on the wonderful business empire he had built up, Cassie thought. A son in his own image. Not me. Women didn't really count to her father beyond the basic and obvious pleasure of their beauty, the charm of their conversation, the buzz of their admiration and artful flirtatiousness.

He turned, caught Cassie's eyes on him and raised his glass to her in a smooth, studied toast. She knew she was looking good. It was definitely about pleasing him. She was wearing the jewellery he had given her for her twenty-first birthday. A necklet of large South Sea pearls, with matching pearl earrings set in a basket of gold studded with diamond points. A glorious present as befitting the sort of patrician father he considered himself to be.

At least the gift had impressed everyone at the celebration when her mother had invited every young man she considered suitable for Cassie to fall in love with. That had included Nick. This was far from being his first time inside her parents harbour-side mansion.

Her father, who did approve of Nick, wouldn't like Matthew. She knew that in her bones. Even if Matthew weren't Jock Macalister's son. Her mother wouldn't hesitate to call Matthew uncouth. The fact was, anyone who didn't have money, dressed carelessly, or drove a battered car would be considered a boor. A terrible sense of loss continued to bear down on her. She had only known Matthew such a short time but he had captivated her utterly.

While the conversation eddied around her she absorbed the familiar scene, trying to place Matthew somewhere in it. Dressed in a costly dinner suit like her father's, his wonderful dark red hair brushed straight back from his wide brow, maybe an inch or so off it at the back, Matthew would easily eclipse any man at the table. Including her father.

No one had the blazing intensity of Matthew's blue eyes, that electric air. Matthew, she had found, could be witty, charming, clever. He mightn't have gone to university but she was prepared to bet he could hold his own in any discussion going on around this table. He was totally his own person. He was a true achiever. He was also the last man in the world her parents would regard as an excellent match.

"Where did you go off to?" Nick asked much later as he escorted Cassie to his car.

"Why make it sound like I've been orbiting Mars? I've been to too many of these rituals, Nick, I can't take a seat at my parent's table without grieving."

"About what?" Nick asked in genuine puzzlement.

"Family togetherness," Cassie said. It was the simple truth.

When they arrived outside Cassie's apartment block, Nick begged to come up. "I don't think that would help, Nick." Cassie pulled away from the hand that had moved caressingly around her neck.

"What's happened to you since you went away on holidays?" Nick demanded, his handsome face perplexed. "Where *are* you really?"

"Right here."

"Was it someone you met up there?" Nick persisted, a frown appearing between his brows.

"If I did, they turned me down," Cassie said in a wry voice, preparing to get out of the car.

"Are you serious?" Nick caught her arm, restraining her. "Let's get this cleared up. You met some guy and he turned you down?"

"They don't do that often," Cassie joked.

"So now you know what it feels like," Nick said. "I love you, Cassie."

"And I love you, too." She reached back and kissed his cheek. "But as a dear friend. Not someone I want to spend my life with. We've had all this out, Nicko."

"Ah, a *pal!*" He stared into her face. "That's not too bad for now. I'm going to give you time, Cassie, to get over your fantasies." Nick stepped swiftly out of the car and came around to Cassie's side, helping her out onto the street. "Marriage is a big step. We've both got plenty of time to think about it. A big thing I've got going for me is your father approves of me."

"What about *me?*" Cassie asked laconically.

"Your father is very proud of you. He told me," Nick said in a tender voice, but Cassie only smiled.

"I don't suppose you noticed I left home as soon as I was able. I think it was close to six months before anyone noticed. Anyway, thank you for coming with me, Nicko. You're always so supportive."

"Can't I come up for ten minutes?" he begged, the old desire pumping. "I promise I won't overstay my welcome." Nick reached out and tightly held her to him. Such a beautiful girl but so vulnerable. Of course her parents adored her. It was simply they led such a high-powered life.

Matthew, watching from the shadowed interior of a

hire car, was witness to this tenderly passionate scene. Now the guy was kissing her, his whole body language yearning. In the lights from the well-lit exterior of the swish apartment block, Matthew could see the man was roughly his own age, maybe a year or two younger, tall, dark-haired, dressed in an outfit Matthew had never worn in his life nor ever expected to. An expensive dinner suit. He wore it with easy grace. He couldn't stop kissing Cassandra and Matthew felt a momentary delirium, an intense rush of jealousy, raw and pure. The thought of another man touching her. He felt his hands clench on the steering wheel. His breathing stopped as he waited for the next move. He didn't care if it was right or wrong, he was going to stop it.

Cassandra broke away.

The relief he felt was so acute it actually hurt. She was shaking her head, saying something.

"'Bye-bye, Nicko," she called.

Then she was almost running. It was time for him to move. He'd been waiting in the visitors' parking lot for over two hours. He had found both her parents' address and hers simply from running a finger down the phone book. He got a recorded message when he rang Cassandra's phone, thrilling to the sound of her voice again, tongue-tied for a moment when it came time for him to speak after the beep.

He'd even driven past the Stirlings' mansion, impressed despite himself at its sheer size and imposing structure, the magnificent position overlooking arguably the finest harbour in the world. The mansion, one simply couldn't call it a house, was all lit up. Obviously some kind of party was in progress. Though the frontage was walled to a man's height, he could see several luxury cars parked around the driveway through the massive wrought-iron gates. Probably Cassandra was there, celebrating some event at the family home.

Finally he drove back to her apartment block and waited. And waited. That was hard. He wasn't a man for much waiting about.

Now here she was. He could feel the instant heat, the adrenaline rush, that flooded into his body. What's his name—Nicko—was back in his car, driving away.

Matthew acted, leaping a small beautifully manicured hedge to meet up with Cassandra before she activated the security door and went inside.

"Cassandra," he called once. Then louder. "Cassandra." This was what he preferred, action.

She turned and saw him, the shock registering on her beautiful face. She was wearing a white dress that sparkled, a dream of a dress, her wonderful hair drawn away from her face and knotted at the back. He could see some ornament that held the gleaming masses. Diamonds, crystals. It glittered.

Then he stood before her, a kind of anguish on his face, his high cheekbones flushed with the sudden torrent of emotion. "I need to see you," he said.

"What can you possibly want to say?" Anger and passion overlapped. Hadn't he put her through hell for weeks?

"Hello, beautiful Cassandra," he said, his vibrant voice a little unsteady. "It's wonderful to see you again."

"God, Matthew."

She struggled to come to terms with her warring feelings. Pride demanded she send him on his way.

"Let's go inside. Talk," he urged.

Such was his powerful fascination, Cassie let him in. "How did you know where I lived?"

"The phone book, what else?" He was desperate to touch her. Didn't.

"You didn't call Julie?"

"Let's keep Julie out of it." He only wanted to talk about *them.* "I even drove over to your parents' house. Be it ever so humble."

"I was there for a dinner party."

"With Nicko?" He had another powerful urge to sweep her into his arms, kiss her, but he didn't want to appear the reckless wild man. They were in the elevator that took them to the tenth floor where Cassie had bought her apartment with some of her inheritance from her maternal grandmother.

Every nerve in her body was jumping. She felt like she was being deliberately teased.

Matthew Carlyle.

They were inside the apartment that she had made as attractive as she knew how, listening on one level to Matthew saying how much he liked it, the English floral upholstery, the couple of beautiful antique pieces, the three remarkable paintings, all left to her by her grandmother. The objects, the porcelains, two bronzes of a boy and a girl she had loved as a child. Having her grandmother's things around her comforted her. She wished she had her grandmother now to give her advice.

"Would you like something?" she asked, dropping her evening purse onto one of the sofas, trying to ease the enormous mounting tension.

"Just to look at you." He had been standing admiring one of the paintings, a magical landscape, now he turned, his blue eyes ablaze against his copper skin.

"You look radiant. A goddess come straight down from her pedestal. Is Nicko the guy in the office?"

"Does it matter?" It shamed her to realise how very much she was in his power.

"He is, isn't he?"

"Are you going to tell me why you're here?" Irked, she almost snapped.

"Like I said. To see you." His eyes appraised the large lustrous necklet of pearls, the fancy earrings, the unfamiliar hairstyle. "I've never seen your hair like that."

"Classical style," Cassie explained. "My father likes it this way."

"So the dutiful daughter wears it like that." He came across the room and closed in on her. He put out his hand, freed her hair of the jewelled pin, then the clips that secured the chignon, dropping them into the top pocket of his jacket, a navy blazer which he wore over an open-necked sapphire-blue shirt and a pair of dress jeans. His body was simply so tall, so perfectly proportioned, so elegant, he looked like a Calvin Klein ad.

"I've missed you, Cassandra." He felt turbulent in an odd blissful way, revelling in the scented weight of her loosened hair.

She drew in a sharp breath, at the same time impaled by his hand. His fingers were moving against her scalp, gently massaging, dropping to her nape, encircling it.

"Don't be angry at me," he muttered, intense desire in his eyes.

"I am angry." She was, and furiously aroused.

"Of course you are. Why wouldn't you be?" He sounded shaken and humble.

"Why didn't you even come to the airport?" She said, a tear glittering along her lashes.

He couldn't bear to see her wounded. "Because I'm a stupid, stupid, man. I don't believe it now, but I wanted to make it as hard for you as I knew how."

"You brute!" Her face flamed with feeling and her mouth, rose-tinged and velvety, shaped an exquisitely sensual pouting cushion.

The crackle in his blood rose to a roar. There was no time for her to refuse him. He hauled her hard against him, plunging his mouth over hers, a wild beating in his ears while he waited for her to yield to his onslaught. He knew it was wrong to force her. He believed, he hoped, he would never do that, but this fever inside him was making him dizzy.

He had never wanted any woman like this. The sheer power of that want had come as a terrible shock.

Gradually under that rage of passion, the hand that had been pushing with such futility against his shoulder, now slid across his chest, her fingers finding a button, working it free. She was caressing his bare skin, her fingers moving through the tangle of hair plying that taut flesh. If she continued to do that, all his precious control would surely crumble. My God, he was so hungry for her. Starved.

They were kissing open-mouthed, desperately, avidly, as if each couldn't get enough of the other. His hands moved down over her body, skimming the beautiful white dress that clung like a second skin, cupping her provocative small bottom, holding her tighter against his own throbbing body. The pleasure was dazzling, driving him on. Cassie's knees must have weakened because she was sliding limply against him, an invitation for him to pick her up and carry her through

to her bedroom. Overwhelming desire tore the breath
from his lungs. He felt as fierce and focused as a cave-
man. This woman he wanted. She was unbelievably
alluring to him, the long hair, the silky skin, the slender limbs. He could almost feel himself entering her
beautiful body.

But what would happen then? He who prided himself on his judgement. He *cared* about her too dammed
much. Blindly he broke away. He hadn't come prepared for a sexual encounter, and he realised she had
gone beyond the point where she was strong enough
to resist him. He wasn't playing the good guy. He was
mad for her, his whole body one compulsive, powerful
dangerous machine, but it was more than probable he
could make her pregnant. He felt virile enough.
Insatiable. Making her pregnant was something he
wished for with all his heart, but she had to crave it,
too. In her own time.

"Cassandra." He scooped her up and sank into the
plush depths of a sofa. Her short skirt had ridden up,
revealing her slender legs pale and gleaming in the
sheerest stockings. Past the shimmering hem of her
skirt was the apex of her heart-shaped body. To touch
her there would be glorious and a potential disaster.
She was so vulnerable, so vulnerable.

It took Cassie many moments to find her voice, sensation still shooting through her body making her
limbs tremble. "You're good at making me lose my
head." Her words were huskily given.

"I couldn't go any further." His voice was deep,
agonised, intimate. "I had to stop."

"Why?" When she was desperate for him to devour
her.

"Why?" He searched for the answer, amazed at his

control. "Because it's the right thing to do." His nerves were as tight as wire. "What sort of man do you think I am? A man like my father? A man who takes what he wants without a thought for the woman. I know what that sort of behaviour brought to my mother."

Cassie sobered, under a flood of understanding. "But I'm not your mother, Matthew. I'm not even like her. I'm one of the generation educated to looking after themselves."

"You're on the pill?" His fingers that were playing with agitation through her hair, stilled.

"Ask no questions, hear no lies." Cassie wasn't going to go into any detail. "I'm not sexually adventurous but I have taken it, yes."

"You had a relationship with Nicko? Is that right?" He slipped instantly into a jealousy that left him shaken.

She pressed her head back into his shoulder. "On and off for about two years. But it's long over. Does that shock you?"

He stared away, his eyes glowing like coals. "I wish it hadn't happened."

"But you've had relationships, Matthew." She felt and sounded upset. "I know nothing about them."

"They *were* nothing," he countered. "Nothing compared to you."

"Then it's the same with me. I thought I was in love with Nick. He means a lot to me as a friend, but my emotions lacked deep involvement. I tried but I could never see myself as his wife."

"Did you live with him?" Matthew fought to overcome this dark jealousy, so new to him. It was something he hadn't been prepared for.

"No. It wasn't best for either of us. Neither of our families would have approved, anyway. Marriage, yes. Live-in relationships, no. My own space has always been important to me. Up until now."

"But you still see him?" He wanted to learn everything about her. Discover her secrets.

"I *work* with him, Matthew," she retaliated. "Our romance is finished but he's still my friend."

His hand slid around her face, dangerously electrical, forcing her to meet his eyes. "Watching you, I thought he was a lot more than that."

"No." She gave a little distressed sigh. "Nick could kiss me a thousand times and it would never add up to one kiss from you."

He released her then, giving his heart-wrenching smile. "Fine. Can I talk to you now?"

"I want you to." She lay breathless in longing while he pushed a cushion behind her head.

His heart thudding crazily, he tried to repress the passion the sight and nearness of her aroused. For the first time it struck him his hands were terribly rough. Okay, so they weren't a bad shape, but the inside of his fingers and his palms were calloused.

Amazingly she took his calloused hand and held it to her breast. "We'll work it out, Matthew. Neither of us could say goodbye easily."

"I should never have let you leave." His fingers moved to link with hers. "Why don't you come back with me to Jabiru for a few weeks? I want you to experience Outback life at first-hand. Living in the middle of nowhere. Then we can both be certain it's where you're going to thrive. Too much emotion has happened to us too fast." His voice deepened as he looked very earnestly into her lovely face, sensing she was both excited and troubled.

"You're asking me to live at the homestead with you? The two of us alone?"

God, it would be *perfect*. An answering excitement was like a blaze within him but he tried to bank it down. No use being hard and hungry. This was a princess. "I'm not asking for a trial marriage, Cassandra, though it's a powerful temptation."

"But you're *human*, Matthew." Her eyes sparkled like diamonds.

"You're telling me! I'm no saint." His vibrant voice rasped. There was a swift rise of colour beneath her velvety skin, a sure indication of her imaginings, her lying spread out on his bed, him deep inside of her, fevered with desire, glorying in possession. "I swear I would never take advantage of you, Cassie, even if it kills me. I care about you too much to sabotage my chances. Obviously it can't be the two of us *alone*. If you agree, there's an old mate of mine, Ned Croft, who could play chaperone or something very like it. He'd be right there, at any rate. He'd love to come. Ned's a real character and a good person. You'll like him."

"So we play house?" Cassie's lips parted on a shaky breath.

"Don't you want to?" His blue eyes smouldered.

"Oh, yes." Suddenly all misgivings fell away. She reached up to link her arms around his neck. "It sounds great."

CHAPTER SEVEN

CASSIE lay in her narrow bed, the mosquito netting billowing around her, eyes closed but ears alert for the early morning sounds. This was her third day on Jabiru and she was settling in beautifully. Ned was a real sweetie, with eyes as bright and innocent as a baby's. They had taken to each other at once.

Ned was never happier than roaming the station doing little jobs here and there, drinking billy tea with the men. It seemed to Cassie he idolised Matthew, and Matthew clearly looked on Ned as family. It had worked out well. Ned had a droll sense of humour, as well, and he was well aware he was there to keep a "sharp eye" on the household arrangements as he once told her in his spare funny way.

It was decided, on Cassie's insistence, she would take over the cooking, something that appeared to make both men happy, so that meant she had to be up at dawn to make breakfast. And a full breakfast at that. Juice, fruit, steak and eggs, lashing of tea and toast. No hardship. Matthew and Ned appreciated her efforts and she was coming to realise she was quite domesticated.

She loved the early mornings. Especially the predawn. Picaninny dawn, the Aborigines called it, a time of magic, so wonderfully peaceful and still when nothing moved except the stars as they picked up their swags of diamonds and left the velvety sky one by one.

In a few more minutes the dogs would begin to stir, then Ned, who had his bunk out on a veranda silvered by the moon. Cassie opened her eyes, threw back the mosquito netting and got a little gingerly to her feet. Her muscles were a bit stiff and sore after so much riding. She had never been on a horse for such long periods in years. But she was loving it, riding between Matthew and Ned as they toured various camps on the station. It was an exciting life, so open and free, but she could see at times brutally hard and dangerous. Terrible accidents weren't unheard of.

Matthew came behind her as she was slicing paw-paw and mango into a bowl, bestowing a heart-stopping smile upon her, allowing himself the luxury of nuzzling her cheek.

"Sleep well?" The intimacy of his tone lent great charm to his voice. There was the pleasant scent of a herbal soap. More luxurious, the scent of *him*.

"Did you?" she parried, thinking her whole life had changed.

"Think of it this way, Cassandra," he drawled, "I'm a man on a knife edge. Rapture lies into the future."

"I'm thinking it will have to with Ned around!" Cassie answered, excited and amused. Ned took his job of chaperone seriously.

They ate at the big pine table, Ned contending he hadn't eaten so well for years.

"And here I was thinking you enjoyed my cooking," Matthew teased.

Ned nearly choked to set him straight. "So I *do*. I do, but it's lovely having a woman around. One as sweet and beautiful as Cassie. She's a man's dream."

"I think that earns you another cup of tea, Ned."
Cassie got up to fetch the teapot.

Later in the morning she sat in the leafy shade of a
paperbark with a marvellously textured trunk, watching Matthew, stripped to the waist, repair a section of
fencing at the Twenty Mile. The cattle had trampled
it down in their efforts to break out into the wild country. Now when time presented they would have to be
brought back.

What a beautiful man he was! Cassie thought, feeling her heart thud. He could have posed for
Michelangelo, some heroic work of young male viril-
ity. She began to fan herself with her cream akubra,
trying to cool her blood. Such a play of muscle across
his tanned back. He had the body of a natural athlete,
wide-shouldered, tapering into a narrow waist, lean,
long, muscled flanks, strong straight legs. He was, she
had found, possessed of an enormous energy and the
wonderful vitality of an absolutely fit and healthy man.
Even after rain the earth was as hard as a rock, but he
was wielding the crowbar and shovel like he was slicing through cake.

"That should do it," he called out sometime later,
walking towards her with his elegant stride. The fan
of hair across his dark copper chest cut to a narrow
trail down his taut torso and disappeared into his body-
hugging blue jeans.

Cassie's tensed fingers bit into her arms. "Well, you
promised me a swim, didn't you?" Feigning casual-
ness, she stood up and smiled.

"Absolutely right. I dreamt about you last night,"
he said very softly.

"Want to tell me the content?" Cassie stared back
at him, mesmerised. This hands-off seduction focused

every one of her senses. Sometimes, like now, unbearably.

"For some reason we were on a yacht together." His eyes drank deeply of her. "The Whitsunday's. Turquoise blue into cobalt water, a fifteen-knot wind strumming against the sails, you in a bikini."

"What colour?" she asked on a shaky breath.

"Yellow. I remember that distinctly. Yellow like a hibiscus." He placed his right hand so gently against her cheek she closed her eyes. "This is hell. And heaven," he breathed. "Arousal without ever cutting loose."

"It's not the *worst* experience of my life," Cassie told him in a wry, husky voice. It was sexual excitement on a short leash. Breathless with just a touch.

"What a super day!" a cheerful voice called to them, breaking the spell. Ned riding towards them. "Just great! I've got a surprise for you two lovebirds. While you have yourselves a swim, I'm going to cook the damper. Got the coals just right. We can wash it down with a panniken of tea. How's zat?"

Matthew smiled his beautiful smile. "We won't say no, Ned."

They rode light-heartedly towards the nearest billabong, a long curving sheet of water, surprisingly deep, watching a brolga flap its great wings in what appeared to be slow motion. Cassie hadn't as yet witnessed one of their stately dances. She had been told all about them, now she was hoping she'd be privileged to catch a performance. The water in the sunlight glittered a metallic dark green, jade in the shallows, with stands of water reeds and small cream lilies lining the banks, the whole framed by magnificent gums. It was the most wonderful natural swimming pool remote from anywhere.

It was as Cassie was slipping out of her cotton shirt and jeans—she was wearing her two piece swimsuit beneath—that the brolgas arrived, flying low above the chain of billabongs in a bluish-grey cloud. Thousands of budgerigars flew above them, a bolt of emerald silk against the burning blue sky.

"Oh, Matthew, look!" Cassie cried out in delight, running down the sandy slope to join him where he stood near the shallows.

"Quiet now!" Matthew turned quickly and caught her around her hands' span waist. "If we make any noise, they'll take off."

She rested against him, his splendid male body clad in black swimming briefs, his arm ringing her as the brolgas turned into the wind and began touching down with a series of running steps like stones skimmed across the water. "How beautiful!" Cassie was enchanted. Now the budgerigars flashed low in formation over the water, their chittering filling the air. "Do you suppose they'll dance for us?" Her eyes shone in anticipation.

"Not while we invade their territory," Matthew said carelessly, himself well used to the spectacle. "It's *our* turn for a swim after all that labouring. There'll be plenty of time, Cassie, don't worry." He clapped his hands and immediately the cranes took off again, racing forward on their long spindly legs, they gained enough buoyancy to spread their great wings. The air vibrated with the swoosh of their flight. They stood and watched the birds until their shrieks faded and the quivering sheet of water became calm again, the surface silvered by the sun.

"They'll move to another water hole further down." Matthew transferred his gaze from the cloudless blue sky to Cassie beside him. His heart juddered at the sight of her, near naked and beautiful. Her swimsuit, a tiny little bra and bikini pants, to his desire-drugged eyes barely seemed to cover her, the brilliant tropical print accentuating her smooth-as-satin skin. This woman…this woman…was the great revelation in his life.

"Matthew?" She felt her blood catch fire at the look in his eyes. "What are you thinking?" On impulse she fingered the cleft in his chin.

"Why don't we make love on the sand?" His voice was tauter than he intended. Hell, this was fabulous, but he was continually on the edge, his passion for her like a hurricane that could obliterate his moral stand.

Even Cassie's little laugh fizzled out. "I was thinking the same thing."

"I suppose Ned wouldn't look," Matthew said very dryly.

"He might consider it an infringement of our deal."

"I guess so." Matthew pulled a contrite face. "So, let's swim. Cool off."

Despite the crystal-clear coldness of the water, the heat between them continued to sizzle and spark. Taking her hand, Matthew tugged her into deeper water, beginning to kiss her with passion and a flicking tongue that licked the droplets of water from her open mouth and her flawless skin. He felt unbearably frustrated, the two of them curling their limbs together until they sank beneath the emerald waters still kissing with abandonment.

When they had to surface again for air, Ned was pacing back and forth along the golden sand. "Are you two okay?'' he yelled, gnarled old hands framing his mouth.

"Yes, yes.'' Cassie began laughing, scooping up handfuls of water and throwing them up in the sparkling winelike air.

"Gawd, you gave me a bit of a fright, that's all.''

"Sorry, Ned, my fault.'' Beneath the water, Matthew's hands cupped Cassie's small breasts, the silky tantalising flesh. The provocation to strip the bra from her was powerful but he had made a commitment. He had to be crazy. But then he knew beyond doubt. He loved her.

Time didn't seem to have any meaning for her. The days just flew, never enough time for all the jobs that had to be done. Matthew as the Boss worked like a Trojan, never asking more of his men that he was prepared to do himself. He needed more staff, Cassie thought, even though they all appeared to be tireless. Everyone on the station recognised her now and seemed to accept her. She was a good rider, getting even better, and wasn't afraid of a bit of hard work herself, though she always wore gloves to protect her hands.

Matthew, delighted with her interest and enthusiasm and confident in her organising abilities and intelligence, allowed her to organise choppers and cattle trucks for the current muster, and selling, giving her a sense of teamwork, of belonging. Ned took it upon himself to instruct her in the art of survival in remote country and how to recognise good bush tucker. Everything fascinated her to the extent she gloried in life. She and Ned were the easiest of companions, so much so, Cassie felt she had known him all her life.

That day was spent herding cattle along the Pardoo Trail which led to the highway and the cattle trucks after two days' drove off. Matthew's foreman and three of the aboriginal stockmen were to continue walking the cattle in, but Matthew had other priorities.

They were sitting around the dinner table relaxing after a long day when Cassie introduced a topic that had been in her mind. "What you really need is wings of your own," she told Matthew, her face bright and animated.

He smiled at her. "Don't I wish. But I can't come up with that kind of money, Cass."

"I'd be honoured to contribute," she burst out without thinking.

Of a sudden, Matthew's handsome face closed. "No, Cassie," was all he said, but it sounded absolutely final.

Ned licked his lips, a little dismayed by Matt's tone. He had great respect for this girl. If she was out here to prove herself, she was going fine. "Why not consider a compromise, Matt?" he suggested. "You could do with a helicopter. You could run the show from up there."

"I can't afford it, Ned, you know that. Not yet, at any rate."

"But Cassie has offered to help out. Aren't you two getting hitched?"

For a minute it looked as though Matthew was going to react hotly, but he laughed, an edgy sound. "I'm giving Cassandra a chance to make up her mind, Ned. I'm not taking her money."

"Face it, son, you're too proud for your own good." Ned scratched his head.

Matthew gave another grin. "That's the way I am, Ned, but it was very generous of Cassandra to offer."

Things were different now. Cassie stared at him. Back to *Cassandra* when he had slipped into the shorter Cassie or Cass.

"All right. Sorry I mentioned it." Cassie felt her mouth go dry. She hadn't intended to hurt or offend him. His fiery pride was explained in part by his damaged past.

Now Matthew abruptly changed the subject. "I've been wanting to talk about tomorrow. We start drafting the horses. The cleanskins have to be branded and the stallions castrated. It's not a job anyone who cares about animals enjoys, but it has to be done. You won't need to come." He shot a glance at Cassie's face. That beautiful bright light had gone out. He cursed himself for that, but he couldn't take money off her.

"But it's all part of station life, surely?" she protested with a renewal of spirit.

"Of course."

"Then you're on." She wasn't giving up even if he did look strung up.

Matthew went to shake his head but Ned intervened. "Ar, Matt, so far Cassie's acquitted herself well. She was great today, holding the line. I didn't expect her to be so good. It ain't pretty, I agree, but like you said, it's a job that has to be done. Besides, it gives the ringers a chance to show off."

"I'll think about it," Matthew clipped off, his eyes still on Cassie's lovely sensitive face. It was a source of some wonderment to him she had fitted in so neatly, like a piece of a jigsaw puzzle. A princess passing life in the bush with flying colours. But he was worried about taking her along to the draft. Tough as *he* was, he hated the spectacle.

"Well, I'd better get the washing up done." Aware of his withdrawal, Cassie rose from the table.

"Let me help you, love." Ned leapt up in his sprightly fashion, aware she was hurt.

"You have a bit of a rest, Ned." Matthew shook his head, reminded of Ned's age and their full day. "Cassie can wash, I'll wipe."

"Might have one little snort of whisky," Ned said gleefully. "Help me sleep."

"Go right ahead." Matthew walked around the table only to break into a mild curse as all the lights suddenly went out.

"Damn it, the generator."

Cassie was astonished by the blackness. It was total. "We're not out of fuel. I checked." Her voice sounded a little shaken.

"Probably a blockage in the fuel line," Ned guessed correctly.

"Gosh, it's pitch black." Cassie put her hand out uncertainly, feeling swallowed up in a dark canyon.

Even in the dark Matthew's hand closed around it. "Everything's okay," he said soothingly, his thumb caressing her palm. "Ned, the torch is just a few feet behind you. On top of the cupboard."

"I know. I know," Ned grunted as he stubbed his toe against the leg of the coffee table. "Got it."

A ray of light beamed through the blackness. "You stay here with Cassie, Matt, I'll fix it. Shouldn't take more than ten minutes or so."

"You don't need to do it, Ned. I can go." This when he wanted to pick Cassie up and carry her to his bed.

"That's okay. Cassie might be a little scared, I reckon. City folk are used to the lights." Ned sounded like he'd arranged the whole thing.

They stood in fraught silence for a few seconds after Ned had gone, taking the dogs for company.

"You're *not* scared, are you?" Matthew asked.

"Of course not. Not with you around. I'm a bit surprised by the degree of blackness, that's all."

"Come here to me." His arms reached out, made contact with her warm woman's body and encircled her. He was so hungry for her. In such need. But starkly aware of his power over her.

"I'm sorry if I offended you before. I feel terrible." She was aching for comfort.

"Offended me." He brushed that aside. "Of course you didn't, but I can't have you making those kinds of unbelievable offers."

"I do have money, Matthew. Money my grandmother left me." She felt a fierce need to help him realise his vision.

"That's for *you*," he said in a voice that brooked no argument and seemed to put her in her place. A step behind him.

"Why are you so angry with me?" she demanded. Sexual hostility rushed through her blood. How could she ever aspire to be his wife when he wouldn't allow her to help him?

"I'm not angry with you," he repeated, realising his own voice was stormy.

"You are." She was every bit as aggressive as he when she was nearly fainting with desire.

"Because I'm half mad with wanting you. I'm sorry," he gritted his teeth, "people don't really do this, do they?"

"Do what?" she asked hotly, clutching at the front of his shirt. Her vision had adjusted somewhat. They were very close, touching, but he was just a towering presence in the dark.

"When are you going to sleep in my bed?" He hanked the ribbon that held the gleaming wealth of her hair at the nape, speared his hand into the freed masses. "I believe I'm doing the right thing. I'm certain it's best for both of us, but, God, there couldn't be anything worse." Furiously, the hand at her back hard and possessive, he began to kiss her in the intoxicating dark as though keeping his distance was far more than mortal man should have to tolerate. "Cassie, Cassie, I ache for you." He dragged his mouth from hers and moved it on a turbulent journey down to her breast.

"What do you think it's like for me?" Her whole body trembled violently under his plundering hands. But she wanted it. Loved it. "Just because I'm a woman doesn't mean the turmoil isn't the same."

"We can break our agreement anytime you want." His voice was harsh with the force of his passion. "Is that what you want? Just tell me." Her skin was hot, glowing. He could feel the tight, lovely buds of her breasts.

"I..." When it came to it, overwhelmed by the avalanche of pent-up emotions and the emotional cost of it, the words dried up in her throat.

"All right, then." His hands released her so abruptly she started to fall backwards and he made a grab for her, groaning in bittersweet regret. "I'm sorry, Cassie. It's my fault. I'm wild in more ways than one."

She had to wipe that slate clean. "No, you're a man

I trust absolutely. That's vitally important." Her voice was strained but steady.

"Even so, I make you frantic." He was an expert now at gauging her body's signals.

"Why not?" She let her head drop forward onto his chest. "Why not!" It was heartfelt.

"It might be better, Cass, if we cut short this experiment," he said a little harshly as knots of frustration tightened in the pit of his stomach. "I know it was my idea, but I'm not sure I can take it."

"I need to know what you *think*, Matthew. Her voice had an edgy desperation to it. "Haven't I proved myself?" She lifted her hands, tracing the strong bones of his face in the dark, blinking rapidly, as like a miracle the lights in the homestead came on again. Unnaturally brilliant. She wanted to retreat from them, wondering if she was anywhere close to convincing him she had found what she was searching for. This was a world previously unknown to her yet its wild beauty and grandeur brought peace to her soul. She wanted to make Jabiru her home. She wanted Matthew for her husband, for the father of her children. Even if the old secrets forced them apart, she would never forget this place or these few fleeting weeks. The understanding she thought had grown between them.

"Cassie," he murmured, drawing a lingering hand down over the soft curves of her breasts. "You have such strength inside you. But can you be strong enough?" He knew because she had told him, her parents had been outraged when she had come up to join him. She had never, ever, done such a thing before, so they knew now the strength of the relationship. Both of them were feeling too much, wanting too much. It was a tremendous experience falling in love, but soon outside forces would begin to gather.

On the morning before it was agreed Cassie would return to Sydney, she rode with Matthew and Ned to one of the holding yards where several hundred head of bullocks had been mustered and penned. These were some of the biggest cattle Cassie had seen, big and wild from their long sojourn out in the scrub country. Four of the Aboriginal stockmen, wonderful horsemen, were on hand to release the bullocks through the yard gates into pasture, all riding good, sound, working horses, geldings of a nearly uniform bay colour. Cassie herself was on the beautiful little chestnut mare Matthew had selected for her to ride.

It all started off well. The bullocks were strong and frisky but a few looked positively dangerous. Cassie decided she wouldn't want to meet them in a bullfight. This was a big mob and it would take some time. "Steer clear of this lot, Cassie," Matthew warned her. "Stay on the sidelines." He wheeled his horse to ride into the throng.

"These are wild brutes, luv," Ned told her. "Some of them rogues."

Cassie wasn't about to argue. Her sweet-tempered mare was in fact dancing sideways as red dust rose from the holding yard and the bellowing of the cattle grew to an ear-splitting roar.

"You, too, Ned," Matthew had to shout over the noise.

"I'm not that stupid." Ned chuckled. "Some of those fellas are right bastards." He doffed his old battered hat. "Excuse the language, Cassie. Why don't we trot over to that ring of gum trees? Matt, he's a wonderful cattleman. Scared of nuthin'."

They watched in a companionable silence for some time, admiring the skill of Boss and stockmen as they contained the beasts' rush holding them in line. Finally when all danger seemed past and only thirty or so head remained in the holding yard, they rode out to join Matthew and the men, taking up their place in the line. Cassie had tried this operation a number of times before and acquitted herself well.

Yet danger was the very stuff of life on a cattle station.

As one of the stockmen was momentarily diverted by a dive-bombing nesting bird, a huge bullock crashed out of the yard and thundered off at breakneck speed towards freedom. The same stockman, thoroughly disconcerted, wheeled his horse to go after the tearaway, leaving a break in their well-organised line. In a flash, the remaining cattle seized on the escape route so offered and started a stampede to get clear of the yard and out into the scrub.

Without even thinking, Cassie, next in line to the stockman who had broken ranks, made a desperate attempt to baulk the mad flight, oblivious to Matthew's agonised shout. "For God's sake, Cassie!" Matthew's blood curdled in fear and his heart began a hard pumping action as adrenaline flowed into him. This woman was precious to him and she was in terrible danger. Curse the mare! Though it was scarcely to blame. With good thoroughbred blood in her, the mare was not used to stock work and consequently startled easily. Now she was bucking with increasing vigour, ignoring Cassie's valiant attempts to control her. The men were desperate to get to Cassie, as well, but blocked by a heaving wall of bullocks. Matthew could have cheerfully killed the lot of them. As they picked up speed, Cassie was plummeted out of the saddle and momentarily disappeared from his sight in the great spewing clouds of dust.

For a split second all was chaos; not a one of them not sick with fear.

Don't let this happen. Don't let this happen, Matthew prayed to his God. With no thought for his own safety he plunged into the crushing throng, flailing his stock whip, cracking it over heads and backs. Finally he reached Cassie who had had the sense to curl herself up into a ball. While she cowered, fully conscious, he stood his big black gelding over her prone body, spitting hell and brimstone with whip and fierce shouts. The men, too, were closing, old Ned's tortured face filthy with red dust, all of them holding themselves together with great courage.

The mob, intimidated by Matthew's mounted figure and the thundering crack of his whip fanned out, their momentum broken, passing harmlessly with the blue sky above them full of nesting birds, shrieking in outrage at the tremendous din.

Matthew, grim-faced, was off his horse in a flash, handing it to Ned while he bent to Cassie huddled on the ground. It came to him with dread she could have broken bones, and he shook his head to clear it of confusion and the odd anger that gripped him now that the danger had passed.

"Cassie, oh, sweet Jesus," he groaned. No blasphemy, a prayer, half terror, half thanks. She looked so fragile, her narrow woman's shoulders, slender frame, her pale blue shirt and jeans coated all over with red dust, as was her face and beautiful hair.

"Cassie, are you all right?" He touched her shoulder as gently as he knew how, thinking if he had been robbed of her he would have been robbed of his life.

There was a moment of complete silence then Cassie straightened slowly, put out a finger and touched Matthew's beautiful mouth in the centre. "I reckon," she managed laconically.

Sick at heart a moment before, Ned shouted with laughter. "Good on yah, me little darlin'" he cried in trembling delight. "Good on yah. Yah a little trimmer."

But Matthew's frown was like a thundercloud. "That was the most foolish thing I've ever seen in my life," he reproached her, swirling the dust out of her hair. "I couldn't live if you got hurt. Here, let's have a look at you."

The men standing around with vast relief in their eyes, gave her the thumbs-up of approval. This Cassie was a regular bloke. She had acted instinctively as they all would have done. Only for the mare, everything would have been all right.

"You've got a bloody elbow there." Matthew sighed, and sighed again, unable to drive those moments of horror from his mind.

"And knee," Cassie observed, touching it gingerly. "I've torn a hole in my jeans."

"We'll get you another pair." Ned patted her like she was his favourite niece.

"Let me help you up," Matthew said, still in that taut voice that covered his agitation.

"Give me a minute." Cassie put a hand to her face and found it caked in dust. "Is the mare okay?" she hastened to ask.

"She's in disgrace," Ned told her cheerfully. "You put up a good fight, luv, before she tipped you off."

"A proper work horse would have made the difference," Cassie said in a matter-of-fact voice. "I'll never make that mistake again."

"You'll never get the chance," Matthew rasped, not looking up from his task of checking her limbs. This woman was his future.

"Don't get mad," she cajoled him gently, seeing inside him. "You couldn't have taught me better."

"All experience, luv." Ned was studying both their faces. Instinct told him Matthew's heart was badly twisted inside him. He really loved this girl. It had to work out.

"I'm going to take you back to the house and throw you in the tub," Matthew announced, getting his arms under her and lifting her like she was no more than ten.

"The outside shower will do. I won't have red dust all over the bathroom." She tightened her arms around his throat and looked into the blue flame of his eyes.

"So it's your bathroom now?" For the first time he found a quick smile.

"You saved my life, Matthew Carlyle. My home is your home. You can't get rid of me now."

CHAPTER EIGHT

AFTER that, there was no looking back.

Matthew returned with Cassie to Sydney, bent on speaking to her parents. "It's the right thing to do," he told her. "Your parents mightn't like me, but I'll have to take my chances. No sidestepping it. Just remember nothing and no one can come between us." It was said with such passionate conviction, Cassie felt the swift tears sting her eyes. She loved all of Matthew. His heart, his mind, his proud spirit, the sculpted face and body had left her weak at the knees. Here was a man strong enough to overcome every obstacle.

They were embarking on a life-changing journey, but she knew in her bones her parents' opposition would be the ultimate test of their love. Matthew had made the careful decision to stay in a city hotel. Both of them agreeing the celebration of their marriage and the ultimate union of their bodies would be the more wonderful for the wait.

"As long as it's damned soon," Matthew murmured into her creamy neck. He had almost become accustomed to battling the demons of desire but they had to cut the waiting time before he ran off the rails.

When Cassie rang her father at his office, shrinking a little at the severity and deep disapproval of his tone, he told her he was too busy to speak, he deplored what she had done, but if she wished to speak to him and her mother she should call at the house on Saturday afternoon. "At two."

How utterly predictable, Cassie thought. She was just another appointment. She had summoned up the courage to tell her father Matthew would be coming with her, but her father had already hung up.

Matthew, for his part, was quite ready to face the discord and get it over. Cassandra was a grown woman. She made her own decisions. Her parents had to accept that.

He hardly ever glanced at his own reflection, but that Saturday afternoon he took a good hard look at the man in the mirror. A strange face really. Very distinctive features.

He'd had his hair trimmed. Not much. The guy in the barber shop told him to stick with what he had. He'd always left it long to combat the burning rays of the sun on his nape, anyway.

He scarcely knew himself in the new clothes. Smart casual, they said. *Casual* at that price? Grey jacket with some sort of pattern in it, trousers a shade deeper, a blue shirt that felt incredibly soft against his skin. New socks, new shoes, the works. All for Cassandra. He smiled at the thought, catching the stark white flash of his teeth. Hell, he looked theatrical. To combat the feeling he gave a low growl in his throat.

Before he left the room he took a small green velvet case out of the top drawer of the bureau. He hoped with all his heart Cassandra would like it. Only one way to find out. Put it on her finger. Third finger. Left hand.

"You look wonderful," Cassie said when they met, so stunningly handsome he robbed her of breath.

"All for you, my magnolia love." She was wearing

an ivory silk shirt and a full skirt that set off her small
waist, sandals on her feet, her long hair caught back
with a turquoise silk scarf. She had such magnificent
hair he wondered how anyone could possibly prefer it
confined. He was shaken by the rush of fierce protec-
tiveness. No one would ever hurt Cassandra. Not while
he was around.

As they were nearing their destination, Matthew
pulled over to a beautiful little park with an adjoining
marina, helping Cassie out. The afternoon sun was
dazzling, casting patterns on the ground through the
light canopy of trees. Flower beds showed riotous dis-
plays of poppies and day lilies, a small boy was flying
a splendid Chinese kite, watched over by his father, a
young couple sat close together on a park bench beneath the welcoming shade of a blossoming gum. A
truly peaceful scene.

Matthew took her hand, strolling to the water's
edge. "The harbour is unbelievably beautiful," he
said.

"We think so."

"Sure you won't miss it? Sydney has so much to
offer."

"We can visit now and again."

"We can," he agreed. "And you can always take
time to visit your parents and friends, Cassandra. I'm
not going to keep you a prisoner." He reached out to
brush her cheek. A shivery possessive gesture.

There was something immensely exciting about being Matthew's prisoner, Cassie thought.

"So much has happened," Matthew mused, his expression serious.

"I know it isn't easy for you, Matthew, meeting my
parents."

He slipped a supportive arm around her waist. "I'm not concerned for myself. It's *you* I don't want to see upset. I don't know that I would take to that too well. You've given me a picture of what your home life has been like. But you're a woman now. In charge of your own life. Your parents will have to realise that."

"I hope so." The cold clear part of Cassie's mind told her that they wouldn't.

"What you need is an engagement ring." Matthew delved decisively into his breast pocket. "That will make a statement like nothing else can. Hold out your hand." His voice was low and rich with emotion.

Cassie's bones seemed to dissolve. She stood without moving, almost without breathing, a pulse beating heavily in her throat.

"I hope you like it," Matthew said, opening up the box to reveal an exquisite solitaire diamond ring set in gold.

Looking at the ring, a full carat or more, Cassie realised with a throb of anxiety how much it would have set him back. Could he afford it? But the eyes blazing into hers held only the realisation of a dream. "Matthew, it's so beautiful. I love it." She struggled not to cry. "Please, put it on my finger."

He took her wrist in one warm possessive stroke. "I want it to be a part of you. Of us. This reminds me of a star," he said with such brooding emotion it made her shiver. "Of your eyes. I want you to know before we speak to your parents, *you're* the star in my firmament. I want you to promise me for *always*." He slid the beautiful ring down her finger, lifted her hand and kissed it.

"*Always*, Matthew," Cassie promised with an answering depth of feeling.

* * *

Yet the afternoon that had started so brilliantly was to end badly. When they arrived at the Stirling mansion, a maid showed them through the luxuriously appointed house filled with magnificent furniture, paintings, antiques, so much it was impossible to know where to look first, to a large informal living room at the rear. It had a breathtaking view of the harbour. The whole area was flooded with light from the great expanse of glass and the French doors that led to a covered terrace with a deep pink bougainvillea climbing the columns. All this Matthew saw with a sense of appreciation not untouched with awe. It gave him a blinding perspective, too, on what Cassandra was giving up.

She had grown up in this splendid house when he and his mother had tasted real poverty in those awful years before they had found their way to North Queensland, where people like Marcy had reached out to help them.

The light was just so brilliant for a few moments he had only a dimmed view of three people seated very companionably on the boldly upholstered sofas on one side of the very large room. All heads were turned, two men and a woman. The men, tall, well-built, imposing in demeanour, stood up and for a split second Matthew thought he was going mad.

How could it be? As his eyes adjusted to the dazzling light it seemed to him the devil himself had materialised.

Jock Macalister.

At long last. Jock Macalister with a dazed expression on his damnable face. It matched his own, but Matthew felt only a terrible hush fall all around them.

Beside him, Cassie went white with shock. Couldn't

her father have at least told her Jock Macalister would be there? But that was the curse of their family. There had never been communication.

Her father started to speak, looking aghast. "For heaven's sake, Cassandra, what *is* this?" For once his voice had lost its customary aplomb.

Her mother was speaking, too, rushing in, unable to believe her eyes. How in the name of all that was holy was Jock Macalister's terrible secret right here before them? With her *daughter*. She found it impossible to understand. Was it possible Cassandra had done this on purpose? If she hadn't been so shocked, Anita Stirling would have been enthralled. The young man of the dark red hair and blazing blue eyes was the living image of the Jock Macalister in a portrait painted long ago. It held pride of place in Macalister's study at Monaro Downs. She had admired it many times. Now the living, breathing double?

Macalister himself reached out for the back of an armchair, clinging to it as for support.

"Cassandra, would you mind telling us the name of your friend?" Stuart Stirling barked. As if he didn't *know*. This was Jock's son. The astounding resemblance made it an uncontroverted fact.

"Don't tell me you don't know, Mr. Stirling?" Matthew's vibrant voice challenged, resounded around the room. His commanding physical presence was such, he was impossible to not heed. "I go by the name Matthew Carlyle. My mother's maiden name. I never knew my father." This with a flashing glance of contempt at the imposing, tawny-haired elderly man who stood in an agonised silence, looking ill.

Stuart Stirling turned to Macalister with the face of acute embarrassment. "Be certain, Jock, we had absolutely no idea of a possible connection. Cassandra has given no hint of any such thing. We've never laid eyes on the young man.''

"Well, now, that makes all of you," Matthew drawled. "My father never laid eyes on me, either."

Until now.

He might as well have declared it from the roof tops.

Anita Stirling, looking whiter by the minute, closed the distance between herself and her daughter, her eyes wild. Stuart was bound to Jock Macalister in friendship and business.

"You'll pay for this, Cassie," she said in a furious undertone. "I always said you were a very strange girl."

"It was meant to happen." The gravity of Cassie's tone stole her mother's breath. Cassie was certain now it was so. She was as pale as her mother and all eyes. "Don't you see, it was *meant* to happen. I had no idea. Father never said Sir Jock would be here."

"Do you think I believe you?" Anita Stirling gave a brittle laugh. "Are you stupid, crazy?"

"While you're casting around for insults, Mrs. Stirling," Matthew interjected, disliking this thin, elegant woman on sight, "I want to tell you I would *never* have come here had I known the identity of your guest."

Stuart Stirling moved to join his wife, anger leaping in his eyes. "Look here, young man, don't expect us to believe that. Somehow you and Cassandra got wind of it. Sir Jock calls on us often when he's in Sydney. Many people would know. Her boss, for one."

"You're good friends, I take it?" Matthew gave Cassandra's father a hard smile.

"Twenty years and more, if it's any of your business," Stuart Stirling returned curtly. Arrogant young devil, but with the unmistakable stamp of authority.

"Why did you never tell me, Cassandra?" Matthew suddenly transferred his attention to Cassie, who was quaking inside.

"The moment was never right, Matthew." She lifted her head resolutely, feeling his trust in her begin to unravel.

Jock Macalister, who had been silent so long now, found voice. "I don't know if this means anything to you, Matthew Carlyle, but I've suffered for my wrongs." Carefully he walked across the room.

"You know nothing about suffering." Matthew stared back at him. "It was my mother who knew all about that."

The blood drained entirely from Macalister's face. "I swear one day I'll make it up to you."

"Don't try to be human, sir," Matthew warned, drawing Stuart Stirling's fire.

"I'd appreciate it, young man, if you'd leave my house," he said, throwing his head back angrily.

"No, no, Stuart, it's me who should leave," Macalister managed painfully. "Forgive me, Cassandra, my dear." He addressed her almost sadly. "What a beautiful young woman you've grown into. Could I ask where in the world you met...Matthew?"

"Ah, you know as well as anyone where we lived," Matthew broke in, full of a good, cleansing anger. "I bet you had us followed from place to place."

Macalister looked shaky and old. "And I've always been ashamed. So terribly ashamed. But in the beginning your mother simply disappeared."

"The hell with that!" Matthew spun on his heel. "May you live with your lies and your guilt forever."

Cassandra caught urgently at his arm. "Don't leave, Matthew, *please.*"

He stood riveted. But only for a moment. This was the woman who had stolen his soul. Now she had betrayed him. Anger flooded him. Anger and outrage.

"I'm sorry, Cassandra. I'm shocked beyond words."

"I'll come with you." She drew closer, trying to align herself with him. Something that outraged her mother.

"Perhaps you can tell us first why you're *here?*" cried Anita Stirling, her voice ragged with dismay.

"Tell her, Cassandra." Matthew sounded indifferent to the reason.

"We came to tell you we're engaged," Cassie replied with dignity, lifting her hand and turning it so the light hit the sparkling solitaire diamond.

Her mother shook her head vehemently. "I've never heard such nonsense. Engaged? Why you only met this young man when you were on holiday, you've known him no time at all."

"Yet he's the man I'm going to marry." Cassie faced her parents with utter conviction.

"Good God!" Stuart Stirling's face went craggy. "This must be a terrible joke of some kind. None of this can be happening surely."

The heat and bitterness of Cassie's anger surprised her. "You've never taken much interest in my affairs, Father. I was trying to tell you on the phone but you were too busy to listen."

"Why don't you all sit down and talk this out?" Jock Macalister suggested, trying to contain the terrible damage. "Life is so strange. A man ought to see his only son before he dies."

Anita Stirling went to him, staring at him with anxious dark eyes. "Whatever are you talking about, Jock? You're a wonderfully fit man. How do we know he really is your son?"

"I know." Macalister spoke slowly, sorrowfully. "You didn't doubt it for a second, did you?" he challenged her in a quiet, pained voice. "He's the image of me as a young man."

"But you couldn't bring yourself to meet me?" Matthew said with profound scorn.

"You're not familiar with all the aspects of my life, Matthew, just as I'm not familiar with yours," Macalister answered.

"*Nothing* could excuse you."

"I can't forgive myself." Macalister bowed his head.

Matthew didn't respond, his handsome face carved in bronze.

"I'll see myself out, Anita," Jock Macalister said. "Maybe, Matthew..." he pleaded, his eyes seeking those of the young man with hair like dark flame. He saw the way it sprang from the wide forehead, the blue eyes, black brows, the chiselled features so exactly like his own.

For a powerful man, how uncertain he sounds, Matthew thought without pity. How miserable. Like a man who had sold his soul to the devil. "It's all too late." Matthew wheeled away, such a cold, prideful expression on his face. Terrified, Cassie went after him, but he put her away from him with his strong arms, anger exploding like an erupting volcano.

"I'm not ready to hear your explanation, Cassandra."

"You're not leaving without me?" Cassie was appalled at the turn of events.

He looked straight at her, his handsome mouth thinned to a straight line. "You know I fell in love with you, Cassandra. You watched me do it. You've been the greatest thing in my life, now hell, you probably set me up," he accused her heavily.

Cassie lost all colour. "No, Matthew, never!" She caught at his taut arm. "Can't you at least listen to what I have to say?"

"I believe not," he retorted curtly, removing her hand. "I'm pretty well disenchanted with your whole damned family."

He wasn't back at his hotel for hours and hours, causing Cassie to fret dreadfully. She had had the most terrible row with her parents and her head was spinning like a top. Where had he gone? She didn't know, but she was painfully aware in not being absolutely honest with him she had hurt and disappointed him, damaged her standing in his eyes. She had really come down from her pedestal. But then, she had never wanted to be on a pedestal in the first place.

Matthew's feelings ran very deep and his feelings were all centred around her. That was a big responsibility. Surely when he had time to think about it he would reject any idea she had set him up. Set him up for what? To bring a father and son together? It complicated matters dreadfully.

Jock Macalister was a millionaire a couple of hundred times over. Matthew surely couldn't believe she had connived to bring them together? But then neither could she forget his pride nor the way he had rejected her offer to help him financially out of hand. She felt sick with anxiety. One thing in her favour, he hadn't booked out of the hotel. She would just have to keep ringing.

Finally she went over to the hotel and waited, sitting in the lobby until she saw him alight from a taxi and swing through the entrance, a handsome vibrant force of nature. He didn't even see her, tucked away as she was, but made directly for the lifts. One of the desk clerks had given her the number of his room earlier, now she gave him a few minutes before she followed.

"Oh, God, please help me," she breathed. "Tell me how to handle it."

He greeted her at the door, stunning, raffish, jacket off, shirt undone by several buttons, a tumbler of whisky in his hand.

"Well, if it isn't my beautiful fiancée," he drawled in a deep slow voice.

"May I come in, Matthew?"

He gazed down at her, his eyes drinking in the poignant cast to her beauty. "As a matter of fact, no." He wasn't what he wished to be, totally in control of himself.

"I want to be with you," Cassie insisted, her heart in her eyes.

"I bet you do." His breath was warm, fragrant with the Scotch. "Maybe we can have a little adventure in bed?" He gave her a devilish wink.

"I thought we had a plan. A design for marriage?" Cassie said, realising this wasn't his first drink of the day.

"But you're a player now, Cassie, and you can spin

tales. I'm not sure I like that. Or whether I can forgive you.''

"Please let me in, Matthew." She took another step towards him, for some reason feeling tiny against his swaying height. "I don't want to hover out here."

"Hell, is that what you're doing?" He put his head out of the door and looked around in an exaggerated fashion.

"Of course I am." With smooth deliberation she ducked under his arm, walked quickly into the room and stood near the small circular table and chairs.

"What do you need from me, Cass?" he asked her in a hard voice, shutting and locking the door.

"I love you, Matthew," she said quietly, standing her ground. "We became engaged today, remember?" Tears glinted like diamonds in her eyes.

"Ah, hell, no need to cry about it, sweetie." His vibrant voice was faintly slurred. He reached out and pulled her down on the sofa, wedging her into the corner with his lean powerful frame. "The thing is, Cassie—" he turned his face to her "—you did the worst, worst thing you could ever do."

"I didn't lie to you, Matthew," she said swiftly, but he put a finger to her mouth and brushed it across her lips.

"'Course you didn't, sweetheart. You just didn't tell me the whole truth. *Big* money. Is that why you tried to bring me and dear old Jock together?" He lifted a hand to his eyes and rubbed them fiercely. "God, Cass. I would give my life for you in a second, but that doesn't matter. The fact is I can't give you what you've always had. What you really want."

"You can't be talking about *money?*" She turned to him in extreme agitation.

"Oh, darling, *pleez.*" He kissed her forehead, kissed her cheeks. "That's one hell of an enormous house you were raised in. Chock-a-block with first-class paintings and antiques. On Sydney Harbour, for God's sake. Who the hell has a hope of living in a house on Sydney Harbour? Cassie, girl, you were born rich."

"So what?" Cassie was quivering all over, her whole body responding to being pressed against his. "It didn't make me happy. While my father was making so much money I was almost completely cut off from him. My mother lived for him and her social life. I might as well have been an orphan. Money isn't important to me, Matthew."

He smiled at her, a beautiful white sardonic grin. "No, darling, because you've never been without it." On a surge of anger he put a hand to her neck, and kissed her furiously on the mouth.

She couldn't seem to fight free of him. Didn't want to. He tasted wonderful when she had never had the stomach for whisky or spirits of any kind.

"Oh, for God's sake." He released her abruptly, turned away as if with self-disgust.

"Matthew, will you please let me speak?" she implored, her mouth pulsing from his kiss.

"Sorry, Cass." He shook his marvellous red head. "Right now I'm workin' on gettin' drunk. Would you like something yourself?" His eyes mocked her.

"No, I'm fine."

"Tell me, when did Macalister leave?" he asked in a harsh voice.

"Not long after you."

"Have you the slightest inkling what it meant having you drop him on me?"

She leaned into him and covered his hands with hers. "Matthew, for the last time, I had no idea Jock Macalister would be there, any more than my parents knew about your relationship to Jock. I simply didn't tell them as I wanted them to be free of preconceptions. Surely you can understand that? Even angry as you were, you must have registered their shock when we turned up?"

He laughed. "I thought you were all absolutely superb. Academy Award stuff. It's obvious to me, Cassie, your parents are manipulators of the highest order. All three of you could have set it up. All you needed was to bring Jock and his long lost illegitimate son together. For all I know, Macalister could be on his last legs. He didn't look too clever. Money always seeks to marry money. There can't be enough of it in some circles."

"I wonder why my father has threatened to disinherit me if I go ahead and marry you then?" Cassie asked.

"Ah, come on, Cass!" He lifted his glass to her and drained it to the last drop.

"I'm perfectly serious," she said.

"You poor little soul," he mocked.

Still, she persisted, loving him, forced to endure his distrust. "I feel terrible about not telling you the whole truth about Sir Jock and my father, Matthew."

"So what was your big problem?" he asked bluntly, his whole body emanating a tightly controlled anger. "You're not a teenager, Cassandra. You're not a poor little kid from the wrong side of the tracks. You're a princess. Hell, a Madonna. I'm half crazy to have sex, but I hold off. All for you. I want everything to be perfect for you, you adorable little liar."

"Oh, well, if you're not going to believe me." She tried to rise, her own temper flaring, but he held her down easily, without exerting any real strength.

"Enough's enough, Cass. Level with me and I might forgive you. You all thought marriage with me wouldn't be so bad if Macalister at long last acknowledged me. Better yet, felt moved to compensate me for a lifetime of rejection. I think he's worth around $300 million, isn't he? I'm sure I read that sometime back. It made me mighty mad. The distinguished Sir John Macalister, who kept his bastard out of sight, out of mind."

"I know how angry and hurt you are," Cassie repeated. "At him. At me." Without warning, overwrought and feeling the crisis of confidence she had created, she began to cry.

"You think that will make me soften?" His voice and eyes suggested he was losing control.

She twisted away from him and dashed her hand across her eyes. "I'm just beginning to realise you're a very hard man. I'm not a saint, Matthew. I'm a woman with flaws. I regret not confronting the issue of Sir Jock and my father, but all my life I've hated confrontations. I've had so many of them. With my parents...."

"Well, of course you were scared stiff of me." Angry, affronted, he cut her off.

"No, no." She shook her head. "But you're the one person in the world who would have made the telling hard, Matthew. Can't you understand that?"

"No. I'm not buying it, either."

"Do you want to break off the engagement?" she asked emotionally, her eyes sparkling with unshed tears.

"Listen, honey, I thought I made it very clear to you. You're *mine*."

"Then you'd better reach deep inside you for the grace to forgive me," she countered with some spirit.

"Maybe I will. Sooner or later," he drawled.

"You're behaving badly, Matthew," she accused him, tossing her long hair over her shoulder.

"*I* am? That's splendid, coming from you." He was angry now. Really angry. Wanting to pull her into his arms. Punish her. Punish her.

"You have a dark side." She gritted her small teeth.

"We all have a dark side, Cassie," he informed her. "You couldn't look more beautiful, more luminous, or pure, but all along you've had an agenda of your own."

She wanted to hit out at him. Her captor. "You'd better stop that now, Matthew. I don't like it."

"Well, let's do something you do like," he said almost cheerfully, reaching for her in one powerful movement and dragging her across his lap, holding her so her head fell back and her long abundant hair fell across the arm of the sofa. He had the crazy illusion his blood was lava. "Come on, Cass. Wouldn't you rather make love than argue? How do you get to know so much about it, anyway?"

"About what?" she said furiously, trying in vain to get up.

"About turning a man on."

He sounded hopelessly cynical, but looked wonderful.

"Go on, you need to vent your anger on someone," she said shortly, vivid rose colour in her cheeks.

"You bet!"

He should have stopped there, but the tumult in his

blood was too fierce. One hand beneath her back, he raised her to him, his mouth closing over hers so voluptuously, so hungrily, he might have been eating her. Her sweet lips. He silenced her in a way she was never likely to forget. However much she had shocked him that day with her parents, the hated presence of Macalister, this woman was in his blood. He kissed her over and over until the breath was rasping in her soft throat.

"Matthew!"

"I'm here and I'll never let you go."

"I never lied to you."

"Hush." He spoke harshly but he wanted to believe her. Even her small struggles added to his sexual excitement. He wound his hand possessively into her long hair. Wonderful hair. Hair like a woman should have, thick, silky, fragrant. He revelled in holding her body against his in an intimacy she couldn't escape. She knew he was terribly aroused. Hot with hunger. He had talked so much about waiting for their wedding night. Hell, it was too far away. He was inflamed by a flood of desire so monstrous its power was taking him under.

She was wearing some skinny little top like a silk sweater. It outlined her tantalising small breasts. He rolled it up, pulled it over her head. Her bra was a scrap of lace. That went, too, as he fell into a mindless well of pleasure. Her breasts were beautifully shaped, spreading to his hand. He ran his calloused palm in quick friction up and down over her nipples, hearing her soft moans. Her face was so beautiful, eyes closed, mouth opened to her sighs, her expression akin to ecstasy. And agony. That was what it looked like. Her skirt was the same colour as the shucked-off top. The same intense violet-blue of the morning glory on Jabiru. He wanted to run his hands up and down her slender legs. Did. It was a matter of wonderment to him, the soft satiny feel of her skin. The exultation in him was growing fierce.

He was momentarily distracted when she cried out like a wild bird.

"Cassie! Who do you belong to?" he asked her tautly.

"Love me. Love me," she responded, her eyes intent on him but somehow unfocused as though she was centring her own overpowering desire, acknowledging it freely. "Now, Matthew. *Now.*" Her whole body was aflame.

He lifted her high in his arms and held her. "You want this, Cassandra."

"Yes, yes, a million times over."

"Then come to me."

CHAPTER NINE

OWEN MAITLAND showed no surprise when Cassie handed in her notice. He had in fact been waiting for it.

"So Jock has finally admitted Matthew is his son?" he asked, studying her with sympathy, seeing the sadness in her eyes.

"Yes, he did," Cassie answered huskily.

"It will all come out in any case, Cassie. You must be aware of that. Not that most people haven't heard the rumours anyway. They've been circulating for thirty years. I know Jock socially. Not half as well as your father. Jock's ruled over his empire with an iron hand, but to put it bluntly, in some respects Eleanor Macalister wears the pants. She's a Mondale, you know, which is to say, an aristocrat in her own eyes. Old money. Not a whiff of scandal has ever touched the Mondale family. As a matter of fact, Eleanor was considered to have married very much beneath her when she married Jock. He could buy and sell them now."

Cassie's expression was grave. "Are you saying Lady Macalister was the reason Sir Jock never recognised Matthew?"

Owen Maitland nodded. "Don't you think it highly probable? Eleanor Macalister is not a woman who could ever be taken lightly. She has a great stake in everything Jock does. He can have his mistresses. I'm sure he has done over the years, but he'll never leave

145

Eleanor. The alliances, the mergers. She knows where all the bodies are buried.''

"So he's a coward?" Cassie spoke like a woman who had weighed everything up carefully and given her decision.

"Coward?" Owen Maitland pressed against the warm leather of his arm chair. "No one could ever think that of Jock."

"Then what would you call abandoning Matthew and his mother?" Cassie challenged.

"I've never understood that." Owen Maitland frowned a little. "But I don't believe it was as simple as you think, Cassie. Jock might tell a different tale. Not that he's ever opened his mouth. But I do know he's carried a lot of unhappiness. I don't know the exact state of his marriage but I do know in many respects Eleanor cracks the whip. Many the occasion I've met him and I've come away thinking Jock Macalister's a very lonely man. Of course the terrible irony is, he's never had another son."

"It's very hard not to judge him," Cassie said. "Matthew is understandably bitter. Especially in relation to the treatment of his mother. He loved her. They were very close."

"I understand she died?"

"Yes."

"How sad. She couldn't have been very old."

"It was an accident," Cassie said, not wanting to be pressed.

"Julie told us Matthew has a fine property of his own?"

"Yes, he has." Cassie's eyes lit with pride. "Matthew's a fighter. He's had to triumph over a lot of obstacles. It's built strength of character."

"I would have liked to have talked to him," Owen Maitland said. See if the young man passed the test.

Cassie looked at her boss keenly. "I can arrange that. Everything has happened so quickly. In many ways its been overwhelming. We'll be married in North Queensland. I expect Julie has told you already. She'll be my chief bridesmaid. We have a mutual friend, Louise Redmond, I'd like to ask, as well."

"May I enquire what your parents think?" Owen Maitland uneasily awaited the answer.

"My father has threatened to disinherit me if the marriage goes through," Cassie said, apparently unfazed.

But Owen Maitland looked and sounded shocked. "Cassie!"

"He means what he says."

"Surely not," Owen Maitland exclaimed. "Parents often say what they don't mean when they're upset."

"Mr. Maitland, you know my father," Cassie pointed out gently.

Too well. Owen Maitland shrugged. "What exactly is it he's holding against you, Cassie?"

"The fact Matthew is Sir Jock's son." An irony when Matthew had briefly believed her father could have been party to the contrived meeting between himself and Macalister.

Owen Maitland gave a grim smile. "Whose side is he on anyway?"

"Not mine," Cassie said instantly. "Father believed if he offended Sir Jock or Lady Macalister in any way it would affect their business relationship."

"Well, yes," Owen Maitland was forced to agree, "it might, but it has to come down to *your* happiness in life, Cassie. You must love this young man?"

''With all my heart,'' Cassie said with such fervour Owen Maitland was touched.

At the same time Cassie was meeting with Owen Maitland, Stuart Stirling was moving on a plan to get rid of Matthew Carlyle from their lives. The whole point of being a rich man was that he could afford to buy out his opponents. Cassandra could have anything she wanted. *Except* Jock Macalister's illegitimate son. Getting rid of Carlyle was an imperative.

At home on Jabiru, Matthew worked himself to the bone so he and Cassie could have a clear ten days for their honeymoon on Angel Island, a small exquisitely beautiful island on the Great Barrier Reef with thirty private pavilions set in a magical rainforest garden, each villa overlooking the heavenly blue ocean.

Matthew, who had been there only once, remembered it as being the most romantic and tranquil place on earth. It had stood out like a beacon in his mind as he began planning this very, very, special wedding. He and Cassie had talked daily on the phone and they had worked out forty guests in all. The Maitlands had offered their luxury retreat for the reception, which was nice and supportive of them, but Matthew thought he needed to make it up to Marcy for all she had done for his mother and him.

He drove into town as soon as he was able, thinking it was high time to speak to Marcy about their plans.

Marcy spotted him as soon as he walked in the front door, greeting him with pleasure, throwing her arms around him and giving him a big motherly hug. ''I've been expecting you to show up.'' She looked up at him, deciding he looked wonderful. Blazing with life and energy. "How's Cassie coping with all the excitement?" she asked.

"She's due here next week," Matthew told her with a feeling of powerful relief. "I can't bear her out of my sight. Now there's something I want to talk to you about, Marcy." Matthew took her by the arm and sat her down at an empty table. "You've been like a second mother to me."

"True." Marcy eased herself back in the chair, beaming with pleasure. "And I want to tell you right now, it's been an honour."

"I want you to handle the reception, if that's okay?" Matthew asked in a voice that hid a well of emotion. "Not a big crowd. I was hoping we could have it in the al fresco dining area, perhaps retract the roof. Around forty. Invitations are due to go out. The weather should be perfect so we could have it under the stars."

Marcy leaned forward and clasped Matthew's face in her ruddy hands, her mind working overtime. "This is going to be so exciting," she cried. "I know just what to do. You leave it to me, son. I'm going to give you and Cassie the best flaming reception this town has ever seen."

"I don't think we could ask for more." Matthew grinned.

"Oh, this is marvellous!" Marcy enthused. "By the way, luv," she suddenly remembered. "There's a guy looking for you. Arrived earlier this morning. Staying upstairs." She gave a jerk with her thumb. "City guy. Wears a tie."

"Name?"

"Simon Parker, on the register," Marcy said. "Seems a nice bloke."

"Never heard of him."

"You will now," Marcy pronounced. "That's him coming in the door."

Matthew shot the new arrival a quick look, feeling pinpricks of premonition. This was someone with something to say. Something he didn't want to hear about, he was sure of it. Nevertheless with a backwards word to Marcy he walked straight up to the stranger with his graceful fast-moving gait and held out his hand.

"Matthew Carlyle. Marcy tells me you've been asking for me?"

The man, middle fifties, dapper, overdressed for town, thinning dark hair worn straight back, smooth, intelligent face, nodded cautiously as though suddenly conscious of Matthew's ranging height and lean, powerful body. "Simon Parker, Mr. Carlyle," he introduced himself. "I'm here to represent my client, Stuart Stirling." He produced a card bearing the name of a major law firm above his own. "Perhaps we could find a quiet place to talk? My room, if you've no objections?"

"Why don't we just go for a walk?" Matthew suggested in a brisk voice.

It came to Parker he now dreaded having to say what he had been instructed to say to this dynamic-looking young man whose physical appearance had shocked him rigid. But his firm had been acting for Sir Jock Macalister for many long years.

They were outside in the brilliant sunshine, walking down the leaf-canopied main street of the picturesque little town, palm trees soaring, brilliant lorikeets flashing rainbows of colour from hibiscus, jasmine, oleander, bougainvillea. A village, really, on the edge of the rainforest but a prettier place it was hard to imagine. "This is very difficult for me, Mr. Carlyle," Parker admitted with a genuine feeling of regret, "but my client has instructed me to discuss a proposal he thinks might interest you."

"Fire away," Matthew said a little brusquely, understanding it wouldn't be good.

Parker did something he hadn't done in more than twenty years. He blushed. "What about if we sit down on that park bench over there?"

"You sound nervous, Mr. Parker." Matthew Carlyle gave him a half smile that nevertheless lit up his handsome face.

Parker shrugged. "I confess I am. You're not what I imagined."

"And that was? Some upstart cad trying to make off with the rich, snobby Stuart Stirling's daughter?"

"Something like that," Parker agreed, studying Matthew for a time, liking what he saw.

"Well, I'm happy to tell you, Mr. Parker, I love Cassandra. And she loves me. Stuart Stirling is just a damn big windbag."

Parker couldn't help it. He gave a whooping laugh which he quickly choked. "It has to be said that he and Mrs. Stirling have genuine concerns about the important step their daughter is taking."

"Indeed?" Carlyle looked down his fine straight nose in a manner that instantly brought Jock Macalister to Parker's mind. "I'm sure you've been told it has something to do with my family tree."

"Would I be impolite in saying you're the image of Macalister?" Parker managed, thinking it was a bit scary.

"I'm not completely happy with it." Matthew gave

an ironic laugh. "After all, he has disowned me from birth."

Or decided he needed a quiet home life, Parker thought. "You've never met Lady Macalister, I take it?" he asked.

"Sorry," Matthew said without a trace of regret. "He must be a real wimp to be dictated to by his wife."

"Lady Macalister is *Establishment*," Parker said as though that explained it.

"Better get on with it, Mr. Parker." Matthew flashed him a glance.

"Mr. Stirling is my client, Matthew. I hope I may call you Matthew," Simon Parker waited for the younger man's nod. "I'm merely acting for him. Passing on his proposal."

"I'm not dangerous."

But he could be under certain circumstances, Parker thought. Although he had a very engaging laugh. "To get to the point, Mr. Stirling has offered a sum of one hundred thousand dollars if you would ease yourself out of his daughter's life."

Matthew made a parody of scratching his cleft chin. "You're serious now?"

"Dead serious," Parker confirmed, thinking Stuart Stirling had a poor understanding of this young man's psychology.

"Have you ever done anything like this before, Mr. Parker?" Matthew shook his head in wonderment.

"I'm happy to say, no."

"Just how many hundreds of millions has Stuart Stirling got?"

"I'm sure you realise I'm not at liberty to say."

"Perfectly all right. It must be around three hundred, four? And he thinks Cassandra is only worth *one hundred thousand dollars?*''

Parker looked at him for a moment aghast. ''Would you be wanting more? I have that amount in a cheque.''

''I'm a gentleman, Mr. Parker, so I won't respond to that. May I see the famous—infamous—cheque?'' The sunshine caught Matthew's dark red hair, making it flare. Like his temper.

''Why, yes, you can. As it happens I have it in my wallet.'' Parker stood up in a flash, delving into the pocket of his trousers. He withdrew an expensive light brown leather wallet, nicely engraved with his initials, S.A.P., Matthew saw with narrow-eyed amazement.

He smiled without humour. ''Let's have it.''

Parker sighed deeply. It was hard not to.

''What kind of a man is he?'' Matthew asked quietly after a while.

Simon Parker shook his head. ''A man who thinks his money can buy him in and out of every situation. Mostly it works.''

''It's not working this time,'' Matthew said with disgust, and very neatly tore the cheque to shreds. ''Take this back to Mr. Stirling and tell him that was a very bad move. Bad. Bad. Bad.''

''I have to tell you I knew that the moment I laid eyes on you,'' Parker said.

''Why don't we go back to the pub?'' Matthew suddenly invited, like that particular exchange was well and truly over. ''Marcy does a great club sandwich. We could wash it down with a cold beer.''

Stuart Stirling's envoy felt both relaxed and relieved. ''Sounds great. Nice little town you have here.''

Matthew looked down at him from his superior height. "You should come and see my place before you go. Cattle station by the name of Jabiru. I don't know what it's worth exactly these days but it's a hell of a lot more than one hundred thousand dollars."

Of course he said nothing about it to Cassandra when he spoke to her that night. One day he might, but for now he didn't want to add to the stress that all the inevitable changes to her life were creating. And yet, though he tried to put it out of mind, Stuart Stirling's plan to buy him off had inflicted yet another wound. Did Stirling really believe he was nothing more than an opportunist looking for a rich wife, or did he genuinely fear Jock Macalister, friend and business associate for so long, would desert him if Cassandra went through with the marriage. It was so easy to misread situations. Hadn't he done it himself until he came to his senses.

CHAPTER TEN

THE week before the wedding was a lot more eventful than Cassie ever anticipated. One morning when she answered the door of the Maitland hideaway where she was staying, she found Nick Raeburn, looking tired and haggard, staring back at her.

"I got your little letter telling me how you were going to get married," he said without preamble, as though accusing her of some crime.

This shouldn't be happening, Cassie thought. "'How are you' might work better, Nick," she returned a little hardily. She wanted to turn him away but he looked ill. On the other hand Matthew was driving into town to be with her and discuss final arrangements. She just knew he'd turn up before Nick could be persuaded to leave and, as she knew, Matthew had a temper.

"Is it possible you're really going to go through with this?" Nick demanded, far more aggressively than Cassie had ever heard him speak.

"Stop shouting, Nick, and come in." Cassie was satisfied now someone had got to him.

"This will kill your parents." Nick walked behind her while she headed to the sunroom overlooking the spectacular view.

"I didn't know my parents were your big favourites," she said with some irony.

"Lord, Cassie, why are you doing this?" Nick groaned.

"Would you believe I'm in love." Cassie turned to face him, indicating he should take a chair.

"You can't be, not like *this*." Nick sat down heavily on the sofa, looking utterly dejected.

"I'm sorry, Nick, I really am." Cassie spoke briskly. "We were over long ago."

"We weren't completely over and you know it," Nick protested hoarsely.

"I don't believe this." Cassie fell into the armchair facing him. "Your only excuse is you're not terribly well."

"Fatigue and shock." Nick gave her a disappointed look. "I feel as though I'm walking through glue. I've spoken to Julie. She explained the whole thing."

"That was decent of her," Cassie said dryly.

"I hope you know Julie loves you." Nick held up a hand. "She only wants what's best for you."

"Are you telling me that's *you?*"

"I *used* to be. Once." Nick pulled an unhappy face. "Honestly, Cassie, I can't believe this. It's not real. You of all people to respond to some damned silly advertisement."

"Julie told you that, as well?" Cassie felt somewhat disenchanted with her friend.

"No, not really," Nick said fairly. "It just sort of slipped out. Who is this guy crazy enough to advertise for a wife?"

"Someone who's serious and doesn't have a lot of time," Cassie tossed off. "Anyway, for whatever reason, I'm in love with him and we're getting married on Saturday."

"Believe me, you're going to regret it." Nick leaned closer.

Cassie put her hands over her ears. "No more, Nick,

please. A plane leaves around 2:00 p.m. I think you ought to be on it.''

"I'm not going until I get some answers, Cassie," Nick said stubbornly.

"It would be an awful pity if Matthew had to throw you out."

"How could he?" Nick squared his sagging shoulders. "I'm pretty damned tough. Anyway, is he here?" He whirled his head.

"I'm on my own, Nick, except for the caretakers, but Matthew is driving into town right now. If you think you're tough, believe me, he's tougher."

Nick dropped his dark head into his hands. "If anyone had told me only a short time ago you could do a thing like this, I wouldn't have believed them. Your mother and father are tremendously upset."

"You've spoken to them?" Why should it be a surprise?

"Your mother has been a wonderful support," Nick said gratefully.

"I bet." Anger leapt and flared. "Did she advise you to come up here?"

Nick lifted his head to stare at her. "She has every right to try to protect her daughter. The very first thing she said was, 'Nick you have to help me.'"

"You know how old I am, Nick?" Cassie asked.

"Of course. You're twenty-four."

"So stop talking to me like I'm under age."

"I'm willing to do anything to stop you, Cassie, if you can't stop yourself. You're infatuated with this guy. Julie tells me he's really something, but hell, you've got nothing in common. What do you know about living in the Outback? You think it's going to be great? It'll be as lonely as hell. What about the cyclones? The floods? You know you've never had to cope with anything like that.''

''Think positively, Nick. I'll survive. Besides, I'll have Matthew.''

''I see this guy as a sinister figure,'' Nick cried. ''He's taken you over like some damned Svengali.'' He was so agitated, his hand spearing into his wavy dark hair, it was standing in corkscrews. ''I never thought I'd ever say this, but I feel like crying.''

''I wish you wouldn't.'' Cassie crossed to him and put her arm around his shoulder. ''I'm very fond of you, Nick. I want us to remain friends.''

''You're just saying that to shut me up. Why, you didn't even invite me to the wedding.''

''Listen, it didn't seem like a good idea.'' Cassie gave him another hug.

''He needn't think he's getting a rich bride,'' Nick said tightly. ''I hope you were able to convince him of that. There'll be *nothing* for you. Your mother made that perfectly clear.''

''And you agree with parents disinheriting their only child?''

Nick bit into his bottom lip. ''If it's the only way to make you change your mind.''

''But I'm not changing my mind, Nick.'' Cassie shook her head. ''Not for you. Not for anyone. I love Matthew. You don't know him. '

''Neither, it appears, does his own father,'' Nick retorted bitterly, burned up with jealousy.

''You've learned that, as well?'' Cassie sighed.

''Oh, yes. God, Cassie, you're not going to be able to keep it a secret,'' he groaned. ''The whole thing's bizarre. This Matthew could be setting you up. He could have known all along your father and Macalister are business associates. Maybe he's having a crack at the big-time. You could be part of the master plan.''

Cassie shook her head. "I'm sorry, Nick. Too many scenarios. Most of them wrong. Matthew despises Jock Macalister.''

"Maybe so, but that doesn't stop him recognising a pot of gold.''

"You don't know him, Nick," Cassie said in a clear voice. "If you did, you'd know what you're saying is all wrong.''

"Don't count on it.'' Nick turned on her. "I hate the guy. He's not one of us.''

"I see that as a bonus," Cassie said a little wearily. "I know my mother got you all fired up to come here, but she was only using you.''

"Maybe." Nick's eyes stung at the thought. "But I still love you, Cassie.''

"Lord, Nick.'' Cassie tried to straighten him as he fell forward and half collapsed against her. "I think you're coming down with something.''

"I had a virus in Singapore. High fever, but the hotel doctor fixed me up. I'm all right, I'm over it. I just can't take this in.''

"Why don't you lie down? You're not well.'' Cassie wasn't at all sure how to deal with this.

"Just let me hold you.'' Nick tried to clutch her.

"Listen, Nick, we can't sit here like this.'' Cassie was profoundly rattled. "Matthew could walk in.''

"Don't mess up your life," Nick implored. He raised his head, his handsome face distorted. "I'm here to get you out of trouble. Take you home.''

"Only one problem, she's not going," a hard voice behind them clipped off. "I don't know what in hell you're doing trying to hug my fiancée, but you've got half a second to stop."

Cassie could have wept with relief. "Matthew, I didn't hear you."

"Obviously not." His tone was as dry as ash. "I think you'd better introduce your pal. From where I'm standing you look like an old married couple."

Nick rose a little groggily, gulping at the sight of Matthew Carlyle in person. "I'm Nick Raeburn," he announced with as much self-assurance as he could muster. "I've known Cassie for years and years. I'm her friend and I love her."

"Wait up, here," Matthew grated, moving like a wildcat into the room. "I can tell by looking at you you're none too bright, Nick. I'm Matthew Carlyle, by the way, Cassandra's hillbilly fiancé. We're to be married on Saturday. It is still Saturday, isn't it, Cass?" He shot her a coldly dazzling glance.

In one springy movement Cassie was on her feet. "Nick doesn't really know what he's saying. He's not well."

"So?"

"I think he should lie down."

"And what am I supposed to do? Carry him up to your bed?" Matthew added with totally false affability.

"Don't be an idiot!" Cassie flared.

"I'm no match for your friend."

"I'll always treasure the lovely times Cassie and I shared together," Nick muttered mournfully.

"I just bet you will," Matthew said in a slow, deadly drawl.

"You're not going to hit him, surely?" Cassie rushed to grab Matthew's arm but he fended her off.

"Go ahead," Nick invited stoically.

"I have never hit a defenceless man, but I could make an exception."

"Why, hello there, Red!" said an entirely different voice. It was Molly, who hadn't seemed to notice anyone else.

"The front door was open so I walked in." Matthew nodded to her.

"Molly, meet a friend of mine, Nick Raeburn," Cassie interrupted quickly. "A lightning visit, he's flying back to Sydney this afternoon."

"Actually I have time to put him on the plane." Matthew consulted his watch.

"Pleased to meet you, Molly," Nick said. "I'm trying to talk Cassie into coming back with me."

Molly gave a snort like a horse. "I don't see how that can be."

Nick reeled on his feet, hoping against hope his faintness would go away.

It was Matthew who caught him, taking his weight, pushing him back onto the sofa and lifting his legs so Nick lay back groaning. "Blessed if I've ever done that before."

"To hell with this!" Matthew exploded. "What's wrong with this guy?"

"I'd better get a doctor," Cassie said worriedly.

"No one can patch me up," Nick proclaimed. "Not now."

"Poor Nick!" Cassie took the wrong path to sympathy, not seeing Matthew's face darken.

"Get on to Doc Sweeney, Molly. Tell him Cassandra's ex-hero is suffering from a virus, exhaustion, whatever. Just get him here," Matthew ordered.

"I haven't had lots to eat," Nick said in a low, heart-tugging voice.

"You sound like a real asset, Nick," Matthew said, a dangerous light in his eyes.

"I've done a lot with my life." Nick looked up at the other man with a faint flicker of challenge.

"That's the go. But if you want to survive, you'll keep your nose out of my affairs. You see, Nick, it's quite simple. Cassandra loves me and I love her. You don't come into it. Understand? You're history."

"You're making a lot of people unhappy," Nick squeezed out.

"That's a shame," Matthew softly jeered. "Maybe if they were big enough they could change that."

Tom Sweeney finished examining the patient, then looked up at Cassie. "Nothing much wrong with him that good food and rest won't fix."

"Maybe I could stay for a few days, if that's okay?" Nick asked hopefully after the doctor had gone. He was soon jolted out of it as Matthew turned to look at him.

"You can't stay here, Nick, much as you were hoping to."

"Just for tonight perhaps?" The soft-hearted Cassie suggested.

For answer, Matthew took Cassie by the hand and propelled her out of the room.

"You're a lot of woman, Cassie." Matthew held her by the shoulders. "Tender. Compassionate. But having your old boyfriend stay over isn't on."

"But he seems to be heading for some sort of collapse, Matthew," she tried to speak reasonably.

"He's making that pitch, yes, but *I'm* making the decisions here. It's not a good idea."

"Heavens, Matthew, you don't think I *want* him here, do you?"

"You'd never guess when you're in your comforting mood," he answered tautly.

"You can't be jealous?" Her eyes went huge. Matthew was everything to her.

"I'll be damned if I'm going to allow your old flame to sleep over. If you're not going to protect yourself, I will. You're my girl. Hear that and hear it well."

"But this is absurd," Cassie said, looking straight at him. "It's only a kindness."

"Is it?" There were vertical lines between Matthew's black brows.

"And general stupidity on your part," Cassie said, with a little answering huff of anger. "I was just feeling sorry for him."

"It's one helluva step from your point of view to mine." Matthew slid his hands from her shoulders to her waist. "Raeburn goes."

"Okay. Fine. You're the boss."

"And what's he doing here, anyway?" Matthew was shocked by his own jealousy. "Apart from trying to persuade you to go back to Sydney with him?"

Cassie's anger turned to an ache. "It's mainly my mother's fault," she sighed. "She spoke to him. Got him all riled up."

"So who *else* is going to run interference?" Matthew flashed. This was to have been a wonderful day together, not playing nursemaid to Raeburn.

"What do you mean?" Cassie stiffened instantly.

"Ah, forget it." There was self-disgust in his eyes and he tugged her close.

"The hell I will!" She broke away. "You were going to say something, Matthew. Who *else?*"

Off balance, he exploded. "Your father sent one of his legal guns to buy me off."

"No." It caught her like a blow.

Matthew recovered, appalled. "Me and my big mouth," he groaned. "I wasn't going to say anything at all."

"You were going to keep it from me?" She fisted one small hand and punched it into his hard muscular chest.

"I didn't want it to hurt you, Cass." He caught her hand and held it still against him.

"When *was* this?" She felt furious.

"A few days ago. Before you arrived." He reached deep inside him for calm, wanting to kiss, to soothe.

"It's just the sort of move Father would make," she said bitterly. "How much was I worth?"

Matthew was determined she would never know. "I could name my own price."

"Why didn't you take it?" she lashed out in humiliation.

That rocked him to the core. He hauled her back into his arms. "You dare to ask me that?"

The tenderness and passion he had felt turned to steam. His strong arms trapped her so she couldn't move. She shouldn't be thinking of anyone but him. His mouth came down over hers, hard and furious, persuading it into a ragged surrender so her petalled lips opened and he could taste the seductive velvet of her tongue. No one could make him feel like this. His need for her had grown even keener, wilder, since he had so eagerly consummated their love. Capturing her in one long, rapturous night when all the love he felt for her came pouring out like a torrent. Could he ever forget it? Hell, he loved her so much he couldn't think straight. Now, damn it, she had insulted him.

Cassie had already come to realise it with distress. Frantically she tried to make amends, responding with a passion that matched his, running her hands possessively over the taut muscled ridges of his wide back, straining to give him what he needed.

"I didn't mean what I said, Matthew," she gasped between kisses, pulling her head back.

"I can't get enough of you. Hell, I can't even get close to you." He pressed his mouth to her neck.

"Soon." Cassie's voice shook with emotion. "Soon we'll be together again."

Irresistibly, her mind, like Matthew's, raced back to that one fabulous time they had come together in a delirium of passion. A night that still fuelled her dreams and made her desperate for him to claim her again.

"I want it to be Saturday *now!*" Matthew groaned in frustration. "When you're mine forever."

"Our wedding day." Joy welled in her.

"I don't want anyone else loving you," he muttered, putting a hand to her breast. "No one but me."

"There's never been anyone like you, Matthew," she answered him.

"So, Raeburn has to go?"

"God knows, I didn't ask him." Cassie rose to him and kissed his mouth. "Why don't we both take him into town? Marcy can keep an eye on him."

"Why not?" Matthew gave his first laugh of the

morning. ''Marcy's had a lot of experience taking care of people.''

Back in Melbourne at the old Mondale mansion, Eleanor Macalister was sitting in her father's study, a dark-panelled room full of leather-bound, gold-tooled books, waiting for her husband to arrive. Eleanor spent most of her time here now, to be near her grandchildren. She had inherited the very large house from the father she had adored. Now the home was used as a grace and favour residence by their eldest daughter, Tessa, her husband, Graham Downes, a young Liberal M.P., and their two children, Amanda and Laura. Beautiful children. But all girls, girls ran in Eleanor's family.

Hardly a matter of concern for loving parents and grandparents, Macalister thought, but there was no male heir for the cattle empire he had built up. He couldn't die before putting that straight. His daughters wouldn't be resentful as long as they got their share of the money. None of them, husbands, either, were born to the land. They wanted the glamorous city life. Only Eleanor would stand firm against him. As she had done from the beginning.

It occurred to him, iron-fisted cattle baron he was purported to be, he was bracing himself for the coming ordeal. Damned if Eleanor couldn't make him feel perpetually in the wrong. She was five years older than he. Thirty-five when he had married her without anyone else asking for her hand despite her father's wealth and social standing. Not that she was plain. Then or now. It was her autocratic manner that put most people off. Not him. He had always been an adventurer. And wonder of wonders, she had fallen in love with him.

It wasn't a love match for him, of course. But it suited him well. At the time. He had places to go. Eleanor would help him.

There she was waiting for him in her father's favourite wing-back armchair, beautifully dressed as she was every day of her life, fully made up, a handsome woman with sharp refined features, an immaculate snow-white coiffure and piercing light grey eyes, her thin hands glittering with diamond rings. The immense emerald-cut diamond that had belonged to her mother, the lesser rings, still very valuable, he had given her through the years. His engagement ring at the time, a modest sapphire, had been put aside many long years ago as unworthy to join the collection. Which in fact it was. Seventy-five this year and Eleanor was still as sharp as a tack, her hearing acute, her vision excellent. She enjoyed splendid health. She would see him out.

"Well, Jock, what have you to tell me?" A stern mother to a naughty boy, he thought tiredly. Eleanor didn't beat about the bush. She had her spies. Just like him. She knew how he longed for that son of his. She knew of their meeting in Sydney at the home of Stuart Stirling. She knew all about the bitter quarrel that had caused Stuart Stirling to disinherit his child.

"I think it's time, Ellie, we confronted the fact I have a son," he began sadly, taking a seat opposite her. He was longing for a cigar, the very poison that was killing him, but Eleanor for many years now had never permitted him to smoke in front of her.

"*You* have a son, Jock," Eleanor returned icily, "*we* do not. I will never acknowledge your bastard in any capacity until the day I die. You have a family. Your daughters and your beautiful grandchildren. Isn't that family enough?"

Macalister drew a deep, harsh, rattling breath. "To put it bluntly, my dear, *no.*"

Eleanor glared at him. "I know what's on your mind, Jock, but you can't bring disgrace on us all. I won't have it. Not now. You've ignored the boy's existence for the last thirty years. Why this pitiful last stand?"

He actually laughed. "Because I'm dying, Ellie. You know that."

She stared at him, never forgiving him for that terrible defection, but still loving him in her way. "You've got years left in you yet."

"No one better than you, Ellie, for hiding your head in the sand. You've been a good wife to me." Another wry laugh. "You've always stood by my side, but you came between me and my son."

"How do you know he's your *only* son?" Eleanor demanded, her voice as sharp as a knife. "Are you going to search the countryside for them, too? I know how many women you've had in your bed."

"Ah, Ellie. That mightn't have happened if you hadn't hated it so."

She had the grace to blush. "You know I did everything you wanted in the early days, Jock."

"I know you always found sex awkward," he answered her, almost kindly.

"Well, it *is.*" She frowned. "Why you had to get mixed up with a child, that nanny, I'll never know."

"So long ago, but it doesn't seem like that," he said. "I've never forgotten."

"How dare you say such a thing, Jock," Eleanor said through clenched teeth. "It's water under the bridge."

"It's the most shameful thing I've done in my

whole life," Macalister answered with enormous regret. "You threatened to ruin me, Ellie. Well, maybe I deserved it. But you can't stop me now. I'm honour bound to make amends before I die."

Eleanor Macalister looked shaken and aghast. She had wielded considerable power in her own right. Now *this!* "The press will pick it up, Jock," she warned. "You realise that. A disgraceful scandal and that Stirling girl involved."

"They've threatened to disinherit her."

"They couldn't do better." Eleanor leaned back in her chair and closed her eyes.

"You're a hard woman, Ellie."

The ice-hard eyes flew open. "Of course you would say that. I have standards, Jock. My whole life has been devoted to you, though I know I was only a ticket to where you wanted to go. But you have daughters. Do you think they will permit you to bring this young man into our midst?"

"Their half brother, Ellie, but he won't want to come. Wild horses wouldn't drag him here. He's proud."

"I know human nature all too well." Eleanor tried to rally but she was in shock. "He's after the money."

Macalister sighed. "You *all* are. It's my intention to leave Monaro Downs to the boy, together with two or three other stations in the chain. He'll need them. But there's not going to be any knock-down, drag-out fight."

Eleanor who never cried was almost in tears. "We'll fight it after you're dead, Jock."

"Fight all you like and stop looking like you'll all be out on the streets. The one who decides to contest the will stands to lose their inheritance.'' Now he sounded tough and grim.

"You'll never get away with it, Jock,'' Eleanor warned.

"I think I will.'' Calmly, with finality, Jock Macalister stood up and walked to the door. "This is one fight, Eleanor, you're not going to win.''

Cassie remained absolutely motionless with shock when she saw Sir Jock Macalister approaching her in town. For a moment she wondered if she was hallucinating. The sun that had been flooding the world so brilliantly seemed to slip behind a cloud. She'd finished her shopping and now she was enjoying a quiet cappuccino at an outside table of the local coffee shop.

"Sir Jock, what a surprise!'' It fact it was like a blow.

"Wonderful to see you, Cassandra,'' he answered courteously, tipping the grey akubra he wore. "May I sit down?''

"Please.''

He seemed to be out of breath and even thinner than the last time she had seen him, but still a man of immense presence. Already customers at the other tables were whispering quietly behind their hands. Everyone knew who he was. Sir Jock Macalister, the cattle baron. Maybe he was about to put an end to all the rumours.

"You look enchanting.'' Macalister gave her a smile that was still dazzling.

"Thank you.'' It was impossible not to smile back. Besides, it was Matthew's smile even to the heartbreaking quality. "Was it Matthew you wanted to see?''

"Ah, Cassandra, you've read my heart."

This was Matthew's chance to reject him. Cassie found herself shaking with nerves. "You know we're getting married this Saturday?" Nothing must mar the great day.

"I've heard." Macalister nodded. "As far as I can make out, the whole town is jumping for joy."

"It's wonderful." Cassie's smile trembled. "Everyone's treating our wedding as a grand occasion."

"Which it is," Macalister said warmly. "The most important step of your life." His own marriage mocked him now.

"You know my parents haven't replied to our invitation," Cassie told him, glancing away.

He touched her arm. "That makes no sense."

"My father is a very stubborn man. He has strong notions about what's right and wrong."

"And he thinks it's wrong for you to marry Matthew?" Macalister's voice hardened, but he stopped himself.

"He thinks it will cause a great deal of trouble."

"He surely couldn't think it would offend me?" Macalister frowned.

"What you think is very important to him," Cassie told him quietly.

Macalister considered that with a lurch of the heart. "How ironic! As it happens, Cassandra, I'm absolutely delighted you're to marry my son."

"So you admit it? He *is* your son." Cassie mourned for Matthew, all he had lost. Now it was spoken. Ineradicable. "You've never acknowledged him before."

The ghost of Matthew's mother rose before Macalister's eyes. "To my eternal shame. I can't bear it anymore. I can't bear Matthew's anger and hatred of me.''

Cassie couldn't speak for a moment, then she murmured, ''I'm sorry. I can see you're very unhappy. But there are such reasons for it, Sir Jock.''

Macalister moved the jar of raw sugar slightly but deliberately, as if he were making a chess move. ''Of course. No excuses from me. It was a one-time encounter with Matthew's mother, Cassie. She was so sweet, so pretty, so loving, I simply lost my head. The next time I visited the out-station she was gone. Just like that. Disappeared like the wind blew her out of my life. It was a few years before the rumours began to reach my ears.''

''You didn't follow them up?''

''Oh, yes.'' A sick look came into his eyes. ''My wife learned about them, as well, and threatened to walk out on me and take the children. She and her family wouldn't tolerate a breath of scandal. But the real trouble was, Ellie knew everything that went on behind the scenes. You understand? The deals. She struck a hard bargain. I deny my son, or she'd ruin me.''

''You really believed she would?'' Cassie was dismayed.

''I've never been more certain of anything in my life. None of which excuses me. With your help, Cassandra, I have to meet Matthew again. I look on this as my great mission.''

''You make it sound as though Matthew's eating out of my hand,'' Cassie said in a distracted way. She recognised this could cause trouble.

''Isn't he?'' Macalister replied simply, thinking at least his son was a lucky man.

"Matthew is his *own* man. He loves me, as I love him, but he makes his own decisions," Cassie declared. "I don't think I could persuade him."

"All I want is a half hour," Macalister was reduced to begging. "Just long enough to beseech him to forgive me."

Surely he deserved that chance. "Sir Jock, I *want* to help you," Cassie began, "but I can't promise anything. I feel bound not to upset Matthew before our wedding. Matthew feels very strongly about this."

Macalister said nothing at all for a few moments as a hard dry cough racked him. "If you could just intercede, Cassandra," he implored when he had recovered. "It means everything in the world to me." I don't want to face my Maker with this on my conscience, he thought. He had decided not to speak of his failing health let alone the unvarnished fact he had six months at the most. "I need to reconcile with my son, Cassandra. To offer him my deepest remorse."

His appearance and the way he was speaking told Cassie a good deal. She stretched out a sympathetic hand, looking into Macalister's suffering eyes. "Let me speak to him. He's very proud. I'm sure you saw that."

"There's compassion there, too, Cassandra," Macalister insisted. "If it's at all possible I'd like it to be today. If you'll come with me, I'll organise a helicopter flight. That will save the long journey and a lot of time."

Cassie couldn't raise Matthew despite several attempts, so in the end she agreed to their taking the helicopter to Jabiru on the other side of the purple range. She was acutely conscious of Sir Jock's exhaustion. He seemed so tired, as if this was his last

chance. She only hoped Matthew would understand.
Sir Jock needed her beside him. She was sure of that.

The landscape seen from the air was an eternal
green. The miles and miles of cane fields, the great
crop of the tropics, then as they crossed the rugged
spur of the Great Dividing Range that ran the entire
length of the east coast, the vast savannas, home of
the great Queensland cattle stations, the biggest holdings in the world. Macalister himself controlled a
chain that stretched from the Channel Country in the
far southwest, through Outback Queensland into the
Northern Territory. Now they could see the glittering
lakes, the great flights of birds that banked sharply
over the water. Thousands and thousands of them. An
astonishing sight.

"Here we are, Jabiru." The pilot lifted his voice
above the noise of the rotor and pointed below.

Cassie's stomach lurched as they dropped altitude.

"I'll try for a landing close to the homestead."

On the ground the heat assailed them and the pilot
grabbed Sir Jock's elbow, speaking cheerfully.
"Steady as you go, Sir Jock. Let's get you into the
shade. Reckon Matthew will have heard the chopper.
In fact, if I'm not mistaken, that's a puff of dust."

The puff of dust materialised into a rider on horseback, covering the ground at a full gallop.

Even with sunglasses on, Cassie cupped her hands
against the glare, staring at the horseman until his image became clearer.

It was Matthew. No mistaking his topnotch riding
style or the set of his lean, wide-shouldered body. He
stopped only a few feet away, his beautiful bay mare
trembling ever so delicately. Matthew dismounted, his

expression so tight nothing was revealed of his feelings.

"Hi there, Matthew." The charter pilot waved, walking down the steps towards him, holding out his hand. "How's it going, mate?"

A few words were exchanged and the pilot moved off to the yellow helicopter a small distance away. He had a call in the region. It had been arranged he would come back for Macalister and Cassie in a little over an hour.

As the pilot lifted off in a flurry of dust, Cassie stepped down from the veranda and out into the sunlight. She ran towards Matthew, holding out her arms.

He caught her. Held her. His quietness more daunting than anger. He wore his normal working gear, blue denim shirt and jeans, red bandanna around his neck, high riding boots, a black akubra pulled down over his eyes.

"Cassie," he said, his voice clipped hard. "What's Macalister doing here?"

He stared over her head to where Sir Jock was standing in the shade of the veranda, a portrait of dignity.

"I tried to reach you several times," Cassie said with a quick, frustrated shake of her head.

"I've been out since dawn," he told her, raising his chin in a high mettled gesture. "He approached you. Of course he did."

Cassie laid a placating hand against his chest, feeling the strong pump of his heart. "Matthew, he's a sick man. I'm sure of it."

"And how does that piece of information justify his presence here?" His eyes were stormy.

"He wants a chance to speak to you." She appealed

to him for understanding. "Won't you allow him the opportunity?"

Matthew shook his head. "I really don't think so. If my mother had lived, maybe. Not now. Why is he bothering us? Can't he leave us in peace?"

"He has no peace himself, Matthew, don't you see?"

Matthew's handsome mouth compressed. "He's never spoken a word to me in my entire life, now he's here wanting some sort of forgiveness?" He gave an angry, baffled laugh.

Cassie's breath came on a long sigh. "I want you to give it to him for me. It's a big ask, Matthew, but I think he's been punished enough."

His gaze softened. "You know what? You're compassionate to a fault."

Cassie swallowed on tears. "It's *you* I want to see at peace, Matthew."

He studied her lovely upturned face, torn between his love for her and the tremendous hostility he felt towards his father. There were tears in her beautiful eyes that bothered him. Cassie won. He looked towards the tall man standing on the veranda. There was a slump to the fine head and shoulders, as though a once powerful persona had lost his great vigour.

"Only for you, Cassandra," Matthew said quietly, "only for you. I really love you."

Her lips curved with the most beautiful smile. "Oh, thank you, my darling Matthew." Cassie felt a wonderful calm. "Let's put an end to all the long years of bitterness and pain. Reach out to him. I fear the life force is slipping away from him."

Matthew didn't really understand it but he felt a sudden tightness in his chest, an odd pity. He raised his hand, acknowledging the man who was his father.

CHAPTER ELEVEN

IT WAS one of those glorious blue and gold days just made for a wedding, the world flooded with sunshine and soft breezes that spread the perfume of the beautiful heady tropical flowers and lifted the heart. Cassie woke early after the most wonderful of dreams. All she could think of was by the end of the day she would be Matthew's wife.

Matthew's wife! It filled her with such joy and excitement. She didn't feel in the least nervous, rather her sense of anticipation was like a bright light inside her, causing her whole body to glow.

Her dress, made by a Sydney designer, was a ravishing sheaf of delicate white silk lace, the long skirt forming a slight train. The sleeves were long, too, to show off the exquisite beauty of the lace, the gossamer confection worn over a slender white silk slip. She and Julie, when they had shopped for it, had thought it perfection and wonderfully appropriate for her rainforest wedding.

Her hair she was wearing full and loose, long strands woven with tiny orchids, a delicate headdress of seed pearls and crystals worn like some medieval fantasy diadem down on her forehead with her hair streaming around it. Her bridesmaids, Julie and Louise, were to wear delicate, summery, silk gorgette dresses, Julie in a misty green, Louise in a soft gold. All three would carry a simple spray of lilies and orchids.

Matthew's two attendants, best man and groomsman, she had only just met. Cattlemen like Matthew, one the son of a Northern Territory pastoralist, the other managed a large Central Queensland property.

Matthew, Cassie knew, was wearing a cream linen suit with a Nehru-style jacket, as were his attendants, the difference being different coloured shirts with the same stand-up collars. With eyes like Matthew's, his had to be sapphire blue. Matthew had arranged that they would spend their wedding night in a suite at the very beautiful Port Douglas Marina Mirage, leaving the next day by helicopter for one of the most magical places in the Great Barrier Reef, the secluded Angel Island, a guarantee of romantic bliss.

Cassie felt like she was drowning in pleasure. She hadn't heard from her parents. She simply had to accept it. Just as she was planning to get up, the bedside phone rang.

"I have to see you," a vibrant voice murmured into her ear.

"You can't wait for this afternoon?" She lay back against the pillows.

"It has to be *now,* my darling bride," Matthew said. "Not at the house. I want you to come down to the beach."

"You'll have to give me five minutes," Cassie said. "I'm still in bed."

"You'll have me right beside you tomorrow."

"You don't know how good that sounds."

She was out and running in just under ten, willow slender in a tight pair of jeans and a mulberry camisole top. Matthew was waiting for her at the base of the long winding stairs to the beach, looking so vital, so handsome. God, so beautiful, she threw out her arms to him in an ecstasy of love.

"My beautiful Cassandra, my delight and pride." He caught her to him, whirling her about in a circle as though her weight was no more to him than a child's.

The pleasure was so heady, so sweet. She went to speak, but he slid his arms around her and bent his head, kissing her with such heart-rocking desire Cassie felt humbled. At last, at long last, someone to love her as she loved him. Someone with whom she could realise her dream.

"Matthew!" Dreamy-eyed, she stared up at him. "The gods have smiled on us."

"I know exactly how you feel."

He smiled and reached into his breast pocket for a small package wrapped in tissue paper. "I'd love it, Cassandra, if you could wear these today," he said in a low intense voice that throbbed with emotion.

"Here, let me see?"

"They belonged to my mother," Matthew explained. "The only things she had of value. I'd like you to wear them in memory of her. It seemed to me they would suit beautifully."

Cassie touched the long pendant earrings with a reverent finger. "Oh, Matthew. They're lovely." Her eyes filled with tears at the association.

"My mother would have loved you to wear them, too, Cassandra." Matthew battled his own deep feelings. "Do you want to try them on?"

Cassie blinked to free her long lashes of teardrops. "Of course. They'll be perfect with my dress."

"And I can't wait to see you as my bride." Matthew watched as she swept her hair back from her face, screwing the earrings to her small earlobes. She wasn't wearing makeup, not even lipstick, and she looked as beautiful as a magnolia. There was no other word for her. That perfect matt creamy skin, the very soft mouth he loved to kiss, a natural velvety rose. The earrings were "family," his mother had told him. He had only seen her wear them on special occasions. Now they were swinging from Cassandra's ears, a delicately worked combination of silver, corals and pearls.

"They're Victorian, mid-Victorian, I think," Cassie said with interest and pleasure. "How do they look?" She tossed up her head for his inspection.

He was shaken by his love for her. The force of it leaping out of his eyes. "Perfect."

All at once she was back in his arms, mouth on mouth, both of them murmuring passionate endearments between kisses. Temple. Cheekbone. Chin. Oh, the mouth!

"My goodness, you two," a laughing voice called down from the overhead terrace, causing them to at last break apart. "Can't you stop kissing?"

"This woman is mine!" Matthew shouted exultantly, locking Cassie in his arms.

"You've got a great way of showing it, Red." Julie felt their deep emotion as if she could catch it on the breeze. "Come on up. Molly is making breakfast. The wedding day has started."

On the edge of the rainforest, a beautiful bright and sunny place, myriads of butterflies greeted them, flitting around and between the bridal party like a fairy tale. Even the breeze blew showers of confetti from the great billows of lantana interwoven with bougain-

villea that grew along the rainforest borders, attracting
these flying kaleidoscopes of colour.

Permission had been given for them to enter the
rainforest, everyone moving delicately along a track
carpeted with fallen leaves. The procession was led by
a young girl barely into her teens but already a fine
musician, playing the flute for them. Flowers gar-
landed her head and she wore a floating ankle-length
dress of cream organdie. It was like having a head full
of the most wonderful singing birds, Cassie thought.

Eventually they reached the spot she and Matthew
had chosen. A small clearing before a magnificent
rainforest giant with buttresses soaring some fifteen
feet high, creating deep, woody caverns. Luxuriant
masses of intertwining vegetation ringed them round,
heavy evergreen crowns of the forest trees formed an
interlocking canopy a hundred and fifty feet and more
over their heads.

On the forest floor it was like a mysterious luminous
jade-green twilight as quiet and calm as a cathedral.
There was barely any breeze but it was beautifully
cool, the air redolent of mosses, ferns and herbs, the
magnificent cycads, the staghorns, the elkhorns and
the orchids that grew from large clumps high up in
the trees, sending down cascades of richly scented
flowers in colours of cream, gold, deepest pink, coral
and deep mauve. The air was like incense as befitting
Nature's great cathedral.

The celebrant, a woman dressed in silver brocade,
waited until everyone was assembled. Then the marriage service began, the celebrant's expression serious
but entranced as were they all by the beauty and power
of this most ancient place.

Cassandra's headdress, delicate as a silvery spider's

web, sparkled in the green light as did her lovely pendant earrings and the white-gold bracelet set with two pave diamond hearts that encircled her wrist. Matthew's gift to her. She turned to him, so heartbreakingly handsome, a loving smile curving that beautifully shaped sensuous mouth. Softly she made her responses, her voice flowing like music. The wonder of it! It was flawless. She would remember every moment down to the tiniest detail. Once she put her hand briefly to her throat as emotion threatened to overwhelm her, but in truth she had never been happier.

Matthew, for his part, wanted to shout his love for his Cassandra to the treetops, hearing it echo through the forest, scattering the brilliantly coloured birds that were feeding on the starbursts of flowers across the canopy. It seemed to him life had been aimless until now.

The marriage ritual over, Matthew bent his head to his bride for their ceremonial kiss, sweeping her slender lace-covered body to him, both of them drowning in the magic of the moment. Now they had joined forces to face the world. Mr. and Mrs. Matthew Carlyle.

But the deepening forest had one final surprise for them. As bride and groom turned to face their guests, the great canopy appeared to split open, allowing a momentary single ray of light to enter this wonderful, mystical, luxuriant terrain. It seemed to enfold Matthew and his bride like some marvellous beneficent force before vanishing like a bright puff of smoke.

"Maybe it was your guardian angel," Ned whispered to Cassie later. "Whatever it was, it was most extraordinary."

The street barbecue was already in progress by the time they were all driven back to the reception. Seemingly everyone in the town, including tiny babies, cheered the wedding party as they arrived, offering their best wishes. It wasn't the grand, sophisticated affair Cassie knew her parents would have given for her had she married a suitable man of their choice, but it was so wonderfully friendly and heart-warming.

Marcy and her team had made the al fresco dining area as romantic and celebratory as possible, flowers everywhere, a combination of cream, white, and dark green foliage, luxurious big cream silk bows tied to the chairs dressed with cream slip covers. The tables were covered with sugar-pink linen cloths over full-length cream, with matching napkins, the tables topped by posies of white orchids interspersed with feathery green twigs of baby's breath and tiny white roses. The bride looked like an illustration from a fairy story, her attendants like moonbeams.

As Matthew and Cassie walked into the reception room, delighted and grateful to Marcy for all her hard work, their eyes were instantly drawn to three people who stood before the long bridal table draped in cream linen and tulle. All looked resplendent in their wedding finery, Sir Jock Macalister, grey-suited with a white flower in his buttonhole, beside him delivered by his private jet, Cassie's mother and father, their expressions for once, anxious and a little torn.

"Matthew!" Cassie whispered, her hand tightening within her husband's clasp. No matter what, these were her parents. She wanted them here.

"Go to them, darling," Matthew urged, his own happiness opening his heart. "It's what's called absolution."

Weddings are times of high emotion, of hope and reconciliation. This was no exception.

Many hours later while the wedding celebration continued into the night, Cassie and Matthew arrived by limousine at the luxurious Port Douglas resort. They were shown immediately to their suite, the sitting room scented with the incomparable perfume of two dozen velvety red roses. Champagne in a silver ice bucket waited, two crystal flutes beside it.

"Twelve o'clock, the witching hour!" Cassie began to twirl in pure pleasure, stopping to look out on a night made radiant by a huge silver moon. "Time for bed," she cried, causing Matthew to burst into a rapturous laugh.

"I'll turn back the covers, shall I? I can toast my little mail-order bride between the sheets."

"You can toast her *after!*" she called.

In the dressing room she quickly removed her chic little going away suit, then, in her lace bra and briefs, creamed off her makeup before the mirrored wall in the spacious bathroom. This was it! Their Shangri-la. Everything had gone so splendidly but now they were alone. They had earned it. Under the shower she let the perfumed foaming bubbles slide all over her satiny-smooth skin, her excitement intense. She felt alight with desire. Her body dry from a big fluffy white towel, she rubbed her favourite body lotion over her breasts and limbs, imagining Matthew's caressing hands. Next her nightgown that had cost almost as much as an evening dress. The softest, tenderest, pale peach, thin as a veil, with tiny empire sleeves, the ruched front secured by tiny pearl fastenings. She reached for a brush and dropped it in her excitement then let her hair crackle and stream over her shoulders. The way Matthew liked it.

Matthew!

In the bedroom with its huge king-sized bed, she found him. His pintucked blue shirt was undone to the waist, and her bones seemed to melt.

Matthew turned and saw his bride with the light from the dressing room behind her. It streamed through the exquisite nightgown he had heard so much about, clearly illuminating the beautiful naked body beneath. At least he got to see her in it before it would fall in a pool at their feet.

Slowly, tantalisingly, he walked toward her, his eyes gone darkest blue. ''I'm going to make love to every little inch of you,'' he warned in a voice so thrilling it made her heart hammer. ''Every bone, every bend, every curve, every crevice. Right down to the last little atom.''

Cassie trembled, ravished by anticipation, her body arching in delight as Matthew began to undo the tiny pearl buttons...one by one....

In 1999 in Harlequin Romance® marriage is top of the agenda!

Get ready for a great new series by some of our most popular authors, bringing romance to the workplace! This series features gorgeous heroes and lively heroines who discover that mixing business with pleasure can lead to anything...even matrimony!

Books in this series are:

January 1999
Agenda: Attraction! by Jessica Steele

February 1999
Boardroom Proposal by Margaret Way

March 1999
Temporary Engagement by Jessica Hart

April 1999
Beauty and the Boss by Lucy Gordon

May 1999
The Boss and the Baby by Leigh Michaels

From boardroom...to bride and groom!

Available wherever Harlequin books are sold.

HARLEQUIN®
Makes any time special ™

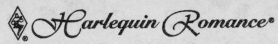

Harlequin Romance®

We're proud to announce the "birth" of a brand-new series full of babies, bachelors and happy-ever-afters: **Daddy Boom**. Meet gorgeous heroes who are about to discover that there's a first time for everything—even fatherhood!

We'll be bringing you one deliciously cute **Daddy Boom** title every other month in 1999. Books in this series are:

February 1999 **BRANNIGAN'S BABY**
Grace Green

April 1999 **DADDY AND DAUGHTERS**
Barbara McMahon

June 1999 **THE DADDY DILEMMA**
Kate Denton

August 1999 **OUTBACK WIFE AND MOTHER**
Barbara Hannay

October 1999 **THE TYCOON'S BABY**
Leigh Michaels

December 1999 **A HUSBAND FOR CHRISTMAS**
Emma Richmond

Who says bachelors and babies don't mix?

Available wherever Harlequin books are sold.

HARLEQUIN®
Makes any time special ™

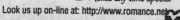

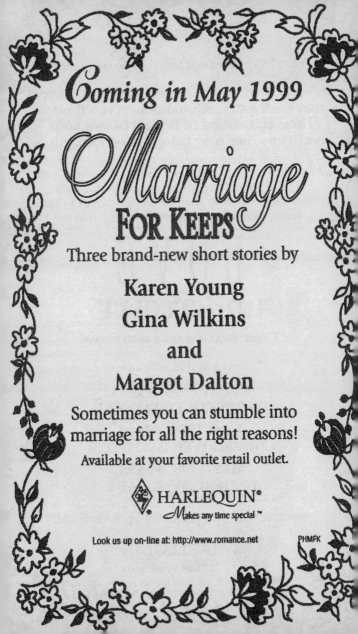

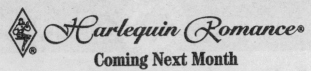

Harlequin Romance®

Coming Next Month

#3555 THE BOSS AND THE PLAIN JAYNE BRIDE
Heather MacAllister

Jayne Nelson feels her life lacks pizzazz. She's just spent her twenty-eighth birthday working overtime for her accounting firm. Then Garrett Charles walks into her life. Talk about pizzazz! Though Jayne realizes he's out of her league, that doesn't stop her daydreams becoming X-rated! But Jayne wants more than dreams…

#3556 TO CLAIM A WIFE Susan Fox

Caitlin Bodine is the black sheep of her family—and Reno Duvall certainly blames her for his brother's death. For five years, he's cut her out of his life. Now he's forced to share his ranch with this beautiful, heartless woman. He doesn't like it one bit, and neither does Caitlin! Only, living together, they discover how they've misjudged each other. Reno wasn't looking for a wife, but he becomes determined to claim Caitlin for his own…

Rebel Brides: *Two rebellious cousins—and the men who tame them!*

Meet Caitlin and Maddie: two beautiful, spirited cousins seeking to overcome family secrets and betrayal. As they come to terms with past tragedy, their proud, rebellious hearts are tamed by two powerful ranchers who won't take no for an answer!

Look out in July for **To Tame a Bride.**

#3557 THE PARENT TRAP Ruth Jean Dale

Matt Reynolds finds Laura Gilliam infuriating—and the feeling is more than mutual. Unfortunately, their kids have decided that they'd make a perfect match! But though Matt realizes that his little girl needs a mother and Laura that her little boy needs a dad, they're determined not to fall into the parent trap! But is it too late?

#3558 FALLING FOR JACK Trisha David

Jack Morgan has been left to bring up his small daughter Maddy single-handedly. It wasn't easy. Then Bryony Lester fell into their lives. Maddy warmed to her instantly—how could Jack resist a woman who could make Maddy smile?

Daddy Boom: *Who says babies and bachelors don't mix?*